"You need me and I'm willing to help."

"But?" Abigail whispered, voicing the unspoken implication.

"I wish to borrow my wife for a few weeks. Nothing too arduous, no marital duties, merely a front for a necessary trip I'm obliged to make."

"What?" Abigail stood slowly, holding on to the arm of the chair, and Logan looked up at her, his dark brows raised in query, the light of real mischief now sparkling in those astonishing eyes.

"You're not stupid, Abigail," he commented quietly. "You heard and you understood. I'm making a trip. For a few weeks I need a wife, in name only. I already have one, so what could be more simple?"

Dear Reader,

This year marks the fortieth anniversary of Harlequin Romance—and we're all extremely proud of that achievement. We plan to bring you fabulous romances for at least the next forty years, as well!

We have a competition and special offers for you in April, May and June Romance books—look out for these! And, of course, we also have some terrific stories for you to enjoy, from many of your favorite authors.

Our editorial team is committed to bringing you the best of the best in romance fiction—and we want to hear from you, our readers, about what *you* want to read! So, if you have any comments or suggestions you'd like to share with us, we'd love to hear them!

You can write to us at:

The Editors, Harlequin Romance
225 Duncan Mill Road
Don Mills
Ontario
Canada M3B 3K9

Happy reading!

The Editors

Borrowed Wife
Patricia Wilson

Harlequin Books

TORONTO • NEW YORK • LONDON
AMSTERDAM • PARIS • SYDNEY • HAMBURG
STOCKHOLM • ATHENS • TOKYO • MILAN
MADRID • WARSAW • BUDAPEST • AUCKLAND

ISBN 0-373-03458-X

BORROWED WIFE

First North American Publication 1997.

This edition published by arrangement with Harlequin Books S.A.

® and TM are trademarks of the publisher. Trademarks indicated with ® are registered in the United States Patent and Trademark Office, the Canadian Trade Marks Office and in other countries.

Printed in U.S.A.

CHAPTER ONE

ABIGAIL watched her father as he paced around his study. She watched the tension in his shoulders, the way the colour flooded his face. He was working up to a heart attack and she knew it but there was nothing she could do to erase this endless fear. She had seen it eating into him for four years—an almost superstitious belief that held him in its grip—his certainty of retribution.

And now she believed it herself, because nothing would stop Logan, nothing would halt the juggernaut of destruction that he had turned loose on their lives. They were to be ruined, crushed, the Madden Corporation was to be wiped out and her father with it. The vow had been made a long time ago and it was happening; Logan Steele's relentless power was slowly overwhelming them.

It wasn't even a clean, sharp kill. It was merciless, slowly grinding them into oblivion. The suffering had been planned scrupulously and carried out with meticulous attention to detail, the icily grey eyes of Logan Steele noting each move like some cruel deity controlling a game of celestial chess. Except that it wasn't a game—it was her father's life, the business he had spent over thirty years building, his very reason for existing.

'Five years!' Kent Madden muttered, stopping to look at her as she stood by his desk and watched helplessly. 'Five years almost to the day, just as he threatened. Trading was suspended last night. By tonight we'll be finished. Everything we have, everything we've been . . .'

He went to stand by the window, staring unseeing into the garden of the huge house that he had built almost twenty years ago. It had been an outward sign of prosperity, a signal to all the world that he had arrived. The Madden Corporation had been climbing like a star, shining and new, secure at last after ten years of hard work and scheming. Now the house would go with everything else. How long could they hang onto it? Months? Weeks?

Abigail sighed and shook her head, the feeling of helpless despair flooding over her again. There had been nothing she could do to shield them against Logan's cold, ruthless determination. She had merely been a pawn in the game, another weapon in Logan's hands as he'd planned her father's destruction.

Kent Madden seemed to be so bitterly alone. He stood with his back to her but even so she could see the destruction that the last few years had wrought. The straight back was bent, the wide shoulders drooping, his hair was almost completely white. He had tried to fight, tried to win—and he had been accustomed to winning. But there was no way of fighting the ice-cold energy that was Logan Steele, no way of defeating the wealth and power he commanded.

It would have been better if her father had simply bowed out long ago but Logan had known he would not. He had known that Kent Madden would fight to the end and he had slowly forced the breath from the firm, watching the struggle with a glacial detachment. Now was the time for the kill and he would not even appear for that; she knew him too well to expect it. He would observe it from his luxurious office in the towering city block that bore his name. He would watch it come over the fax. He would tear off the report, crumble it in his long, strong fingers and it would all be over.

Abigail looked at her father with dread. What would he do then? How would he recover from this silent battle to the death? The last few years had almost turned him into an old man and she knew that when the end came, when the news of the crash was blazoned across the papers, Kent Madden's life would be finished.

Already he had handed the office over to her—not in any formal way but simply by not being there. It was months since he had even set foot in the door. The board meetings, the daily dealings with each crisis had become Abigail's problem. He was too ill to face work. One day at the office would probably kill him.

'I'll have to go,' she said quietly. 'Today of all days, I've got to be in the office.'

'There'll be no miracle, Abigail,' he muttered without turning. 'Miracles only happen for Logan Steele. There's nothing you can do.'

'I know. All the same, I should be there.'

She left and went out to her car. Her father was still standing by the window but he was staring into space, never even looking down at her. It would take a miracle to save them and she knew it. And miracles didn't *happen* for Logan. He made them happen. Logan made everything happen and anyone who stood in his way was hurt. Who should know that better than she did? She still felt the pain.

'You've got two meetings this morning, Abigail,' Martha Bates said as Abigail walked in. 'This afternoon you've got to see Jenkinson's manager and the man from the bank. There's a list of calls on your desk. The phone never stops ringing.'

'Are you surprised?' Abigail sighed, leaning against Martha's desk and looking down at the growing list of appointments.

'I'm sorry. Really I am,' Martha said sympathetically. She had been Kent's private secretary for twenty years and she knew that this was the end—everyone knew. It was not something that could be hidden or glossed over. Abigail smiled ruefully into the kindly, middle-aged face and nodded.

'I know. Thanks. It's all going to be so much old news soon.'

'There's nothing you can do?' Martha asked hopefully, and Abigail looked at her wryly.

'I could stand and scream, break a few windows. Care to help?'

It was funny how even at the worst of times people could laugh, Martha thought as she watched Abigail walk down the long passage to her office. She never ceased to be delighted by the look of Kent Madden's daughter. The long, glossy black hair hadn't changed since she had come here nearly seven years ago. Nobody deserved to take the beating she was taking now. She was too young, too beautiful, too sweet to face this daily battleground. Kent should have been here, fighting it to the end. Abigail had suffered enough.

The phone rang and Martha picked it up, her softened expression hardening.

'There will be no statement issued to the Press today,' she stated starchily. 'No, the chairman is not in the offices at the moment.' She put the phone down angrily. While she was here she would protect Abigail from vultures. It was the only help she could give.

With the door closed behind her, Abigail sank to the chair by the desk—her desk now, because if she had not been here there would have been nobody at all in this office with his name engraved on the outer door. 'Kent Madden. Chairman.' The gold signs were up on other doors too. 'Vice-Chairman', 'General Manager', 'Boardroom'.

It was the last sign that always stuck in her mind because that was where she had first seen Logan. She had seen him at that door as he'd been on his way out, five years ago, when she had been nineteen. Now she felt old, worn out, defeated. Abigail leaned back and closed her eyes, too dejected even to begin planning the afternoon's meetings.

What was there to plan? Each meeting would have a predictable conclusion. The suppliers were edgy and anxious. The bank was preparing to pull the rug out from under the firm's feet. Their shares had been suspended since last night. End of story. There was nothing to say, nothing to do. It was over and it was almost a relief. Logan was just waiting to administer the *coup de grâce*, the final, glittering strike. It would be a blessing.

She looked down at her hands, at the delicate length of her fingers, and the glitter there caught her eye. A wedding band—another of his plans, well thought-out and meticulously executed. She frowned at it, her green eyes narrowed and angry. She had never taken it off. It had served to remind her of her own stupidity, to warn her when any other man had tried to charm her.

Why was there nothing she could do? She was Logan's *wife*! It gave her no rights but she had never expected any. It gave her a voice, though. Abigail picked up the phone and spoke to Martha firmly.

'Cancel all my appointments for the day. I have something to do and it won't wait.'

'Are you going to see...? Shall I help...? What can I do?' Martha asked uneasily.

'You can't do anything,' Abigail snapped, 'and neither can I, but I'm going to settle this today. I'm not going to win but I'm damned if I'll go down whimpering!'

'Attagirl!' Martha chortled. 'Leave the office to me. Let me know if...'

'It will be bad news,' Abigail warned, 'but at least it will be news. We've died slowly for long enough.'

She left by the back way, making her way to the taxi rank on the corner. If anyone was waiting at the front to waylay her they had a long wait ahead of them. What had she to lose? Pretty soon there would be nothing anyway and she was tired of struggling in silence. It was like cowering in a corner. This morning she hadn't been able to eat. She had left her dinner last night too. She was not hungry, though. She was slowly shrivelling up inside and she was not going to do that.

The taxi dropped her opposite an office block that dominated the whole road. In spite of its height it was tasteful, the stone of the facing blending in with the older buildings around it. But there was no mistaking it. One word—one name—served as a reminder of the man who held them in the palm of his hand and that name swept across the front of the building in letters six feet high. She had to look up to see it but she already knew it was there. The letters were burnished by the sunlight and shone back at her, hurting her eyes.

'Steele'. Nothing more, just the one name—Logan's name, her name. She clenched her teeth and crossed the road, marching up the three shallow steps and walking in through the gleaming glass doors. She had not come to throw down the gauntlet, she had come to capitulate, but afterwards Logan would know she had been there.

She was no longer a shy, bewildered girl of nineteen and, whatever happened, she was determined that he would not forget this visit.

'I wish to see Mr Steele!' At the reception desk she faced the young woman with a look of determination, knowing that she would be unlikely to get further with soft words. The girl was new and Abigail wondered how many more changes Logan had made.

'Unless you have an appointment—'

'I do not have an appointment. However, I intend to see him. Please ring his office.'

'I'm sorry. It's out of the question.'

Abigail wasted no more words. She marched across the foyer and into the lift. She knew exactly where Logan's office was and nobody was going to stop her gaining entrance. The girl raced across but the doors of the lift closed and Abigail was on her way.

As the lift stopped on the third floor she stepped out and faced the gasping receptionist, who had obviously flown up the stairs to cut her off.

'You cannot see Mr Steele!' The girl was red-faced for more than one reason. There was her breathless state, her extreme annoyance but, more than that, there was a door just opening as a tall, dark-haired man showed out his visitor.

'Oh, yes, I *can* see Mr Steele,' Abigail announced sharply. 'I don't think I need an appointment. I'm his wife.'

The two men at the door turned at the sound of her voice and the tall, dark-haired man looked at her with impossibly clear grey eyes, his mouth hardening as he saw her. For a moment he simply stared at her coldly and then the hard, well-shaped lips twisted in a sardonic smile.

'Hello, Abigail,' he said softly. 'Come right in.'

He nodded casually to his visitor, aimed a stare of dismissal at the receptionist and motioned Abigail into his office with one smooth sweep of his hand. She didn't look at him as she passed, and he closed the door, walking to his desk immediately.

'So what can I do for you, Abigail?'

'Nothing!' she bit out. 'I'm not in the habit of begging.'

'No. I realise that you're now an efficient, brisk female. I've kept my eyes on you over the years.'

He turned to face her and Abigail felt a shock that almost wiped the defiance from her face. The tall, lithe body was the same. The dark brown hair was the same, still shining with health, still showing immaculate grooming. But there the likeness to the Logan she remembered faded. If she had changed why had she expected that Logan would still look the same? He was hardened beyond belief.

His grey eyes were now cold as frosted crystal. The well-shaped mouth was hard and his face showed no sign of humanity at all. The memory of his expressions flashed across her mind—his mocking humour, his amused astonishment, his coaxing sensuality. Everything was gone and his coldly handsome face might just as well have been carved from rock.

'All you know about me is the end result of the havoc you've caused!' Abigail snapped, forcing herself back into the defiant frame of mind, making herself remember just what Logan was.

'I know more than you imagine,' he stated icily. 'And there is no havoc. Havoc suggests a random and haphazard method of destruction. It suggests confusion and

disorder, a shambles. I do not act in any random manner.
I plan.'

'You plan very well,' Abigail congratulated him sarcastically. 'You've crushed the Madden Corporation;
we're finished.'

'Not quite,' he murmured, his brilliantly clear eyes
raking over her. 'The firm is still a viable entity.' He
turned to his desk, sitting down and indicating a chair
for her. 'However,' he continued, 'you have assured me
that you are not here to beg. So, once again, what can
I do for you, Abigail?'

'Nothing!' she snapped out furiously. 'Nothing at all.
We surrender. I'm here to tell you that. You can bring
the sword down now, make the final cut. You've hurt
us all you can.'

He leaned back in his chair and stared at her discon-
certingly, his eyes roaming over her with cold appraisal,
lingering on the glossy black hair that curled around her
shoulders, moving over her slender figure in the choc-
olate-coloured suit. His gaze returned to her face, moving
slowly over every beautiful feature and stopping at the
blazing green of her eyes as he noted the resentment at
this minute inspection.

'You were never included in this,' he reminded her
quietly.

'No?' she queried scornfully. 'I was a pawn, another
thing to take from the Madden Corporation. That sounds
very much like inclusion to me. I was stupid, gullible
and useful. Well, you've done your worst. This will kill
my father. I expect that's what you want.'

'I do not!' Logan rasped, his eyes burning like fire
on ice. 'But even if I did I would be justified. Kent
Madden killed my father *and* my mother!'

'You're lying!' Abigail felt shakily for the chair and sat down, staring at him in horror, but he looked back at her unfeelingly, the blazing fire dying out of his eyes.

'I've never found it necessary to lie. Did he never tell you, Abigail? Ask him! Ask your father what this is all about. Did you think it was because of you, because you left me and ran home to Daddy? You imagine you're important enough to cause this devastation? Ask him why I'm crushing him slowly. Ask him why I'm steadily squeezing the life out of the firm. And remind him about John Steele and his wife, Kathleen—my father and mother!'

'It's not true!' Abigail whispered, looking at him in horror. 'You're saying it to justify everything you've done. You would have told me before; when we were married you would have—!'

'You were never involved,' he assured her calmly, his eyes never leaving her desperate face. 'It was a battle that did not concern you. It is—and always was—a battle with your father. I wanted you. I took you away from a villain. And as to "when we were married" we're *still* married. You announced that as you arrived here.'

'My father is not a villain,' Abigail managed in an almost pleading voice, but his face did not soften.

'Oh, the law will never catch him,' Logan said harshly. 'He was too clever for that.' He lowered his voice to a softly menacing murmur. 'But I didn't need the law. *I've* caught him. He was never meant to escape. It's taken me five years. Promises to keep, Abigail. I'm glad you didn't come to plead, because it would have been useless. I have him right where I want him—my hands round his throat.'

Abigail got slowly to her feet, her eyes not leaving him. She didn't know him. She had never known him and this was the man she had loved deeply, helplessly. His voice was alarming, so quietly threatening that she felt a rush of fear for her father. It was not the end. Logan had planned something else. She stared at him with frightened eyes and then she fell to the carpet in a deep faint.

When she came round she was in Logan's arms and a woman was just hurrying in through the door.

'She fainted,' Logan said sharply. 'I'll bring her to the first-aid room.'

'I'm all right,' Abigail managed to whisper. 'You can put me down now, thank you.'

'Such gentle manners,' Logan muttered disparagingly. 'But then, you always did have that sweet nature. You're not all right, Abigail. Contrary to popular fiction, people do not faint with either horror or disgust. You go to the bed in the first-aid room.'

It was useless to argue. She knew him too well for that and she shivered at the realisation that she was in his arms after so long. Once, it had been where she'd always longed to be. Now the feel of his arms frightened her.

'I can walk,' she insisted, but he simply ignored her, and in a few seconds he was walking through a door and placing her on a small, white-sheeted bed as the woman hovered over her and took off her shoes.

'See that she stays there,' Logan ordered, and the woman nodded her agreement as he turned and walked out of the room.

'A little sleep,' she murmured in a pacifying voice, beginning to remove Abigail's jacket. 'He won't countenance letting you go yet,' she added as Abigail protested and tried to get up. 'Just rest, please, Mrs Steele. It will save a lot of trouble and you do look very pale.'

Abigail subsided, wondering how much the people in these offices knew about her, about Logan's private life, about his deadly attack on her father. Did they know that she was Kent Madden's daughter? Did they know that he was being slowly crushed by Logan? Already her name had filtered round the building, it seemed. What else were they talking about?

She was soon just in her white slip, the sheets drawn over her, and the woman sighed thankfully.

'Just rest,' she said in a pleading voice. 'If you're asleep when he comes back in he'll be satisfied.'

Abigail closed her eyes to escape from further conversation—and Logan would not come back in, she thought. He would now be entirely occupied with something else, his memory of her small fainting spell merely an irritated edge to his hard mouth. She felt light-headed, almost afraid to keep her eyes closed, and she knew that Logan was right. It had not been horror or anything else that had made her faint. She hadn't eaten properly for days. She was light-headed from hunger and tension.

She slept, in spite of her determination to remain awake, and as she opened her eyes a little later she was startled to find Logan in the room, looking down at her with cool detachment.

'When did you last eat?' he asked coldly. 'Don't bother to lie. Your skin looks transparent. You've lost weight. You're practically withering away.'

'Are you surprised?' she began, trying to sit up. He pushed her down to the pillows, his hand against her shoulder.

'Answer my question,' he grated. 'When did you eat?'

'I don't know. I can't remember. Yesterday—perhaps. Yesterday lunchtime, I think. I'm not sure.'

'You'll eat now,' he ordered, his hand coming to her back as he helped her to sit up. 'Get dressed. There's some soup ready for you. It's about all you can take after a spell of starvation.'

'I don't need your help,' Abigail managed to snap, sitting, but pulling the sheets to her neck. 'I'm capable of feeding myself in my own good time. If you'll leave, I'll get dressed.'

Logan's face twisted in anger, his hand coming out to tear the sheets from her grasp.

'Get dressed!' he ordered harshly. 'I've seen you in far less than you're wearing now. I've touched every inch of you. Don't get coy with me, Abigail. When you're dressed I'll take you through to the dining room. You will eat before you leave this building, otherwise you'll not leave at all.'

She felt too shaken to argue and she slid from the bed, reaching for her skirt and blouse, trying to pretend that Logan wasn't there. In any case, he had moved to stand by the window and glare down into the street, his hands in his pockets, his whole demeanour one of rage.

'I'm ready.' Her quiet announcement had him turning round, his eyes running coldly over her, and then he came forward and opened the door, leading the way to another room, where a table was set for her and a bowl of hot soup had just been brought.

It was not a big room but it was luxurious and Abigail glanced round surreptitiously.

'The executive dining room,' Logan growled. 'This was done two years ago, long after you fled. It's small but cosy. You can eat. Nobody is about to burst in here.'

Who would dare? she thought. Logan was here. He looked as if he was going to stay, too. He sat opposite and just stared at her unwaveringly and Abigail found it impossible to eat.

'I—I can't eat,' she began, and, if anything, Logan's lips tightened even more.

'You'll eat,' he ordered. 'If you do not, then you'll still be here in the morning and soup will be brought to you every half-hour during that time.'

'You can't do this!' Abigail protested. 'You have no right whatever to—'

'Might is right,' Logan reminded her shortly. 'Eat your soup. If my presence spoils your appetite then I'll go out for a while, but escape is impossible. You came here demanding entrance to my office. You announced your marital status and the whole building is quivering with anticipation. I would know before you even got to the lift.'

He stood and walked out and Abigail stared after him anxiously. Coming here had been a mistake. She knew instinctively that she had made a false move in this deadly game. She had reminded Logan of her existence and if he could make further use of her possibilities he would do so without hesitation. That was why he was making her stay.

She turned her attention to the soup. Now that he was not sitting there looking at her she felt the pangs of hunger. It was delicious soup anyway and she buttered the hot rolls and ate—it was the first time she had eaten in ages. She had not been lying when she had told Logan that she could not remember when she had last eaten. The days seemed to have rolled into one and all she could remember was hot coffee, morning, noon and night.

With the usual immaculate timing he came back in as she finished and Abigail stood and faced him defiantly.

'I've eaten as ordered and now I'll leave,' she said tightly.

'And why not?' Logan drawled sardonically. 'After all, you've accomplished what you set out to do.'

'What do you mean?' She stared at him angrily. Was he suggesting that she had come here to faint and get his sympathy? She knew him better than that. He had no sympathy at all, especially not with her.

'You came to announce your surrender.' He gave her an ironical look as her face flushed slightly. 'I'll rephrase that. You came to announce your father's surrender.'

'My father and I are in this together,' Abigail reminded him sharply, and his eyes narrowed dangerously, the cold grey glittering like ice.

'Oh, no, you're not,' he rasped. 'You were never in it. You may have become a trainee high-flyer over the past four years but, believe me, you don't even know the first thing about being "in this". You've never had your beautiful toes in the mud.'

'Not even when I was married to you?' Abigail asked scathingly, and he looked at her for a second with disconcerting hostility before his lips twisted in cold amusement.

'Your feet hardly touched the floor. You were in my arms for most of the time. Memory is such an elusive thing.' He opened the door as she was struggling to regain her anger and composure. 'Time to go, Abigail. This way.'

It became apparent that he was taking her outside and that would give him time for more comments. Abigail set her lips firmly and walked stiffly beside him. Neither of them spoke in the lift and it was only as he was actually opening the door to the street that she thought about a taxi.

'I didn't bring my car. I'll phone for a taxi.'

'You don't need one,' Logan informed her implacably. 'I intended to take you back in any case. This saves me the trouble of having to send your car round later.'

A dark Jaguar slid to a halt in front of them and a smiling youth stepped out and opened the passenger door for Abigail as Logan took the wheel. It was done so smoothly that she barely had time to think.

'This is not necessary.'

'I decided that it is,' Logan murmured, not even glancing at her as the long car slipped smoothly into the traffic. 'It's a long time since I drove past the Madden offices. Five years almost. It will be—interesting.'

'The place will be yours soon,' Abigail reminded him in a choked voice. Suddenly she couldn't speak. It was too overwhelming. Sitting in this car with Logan brought back so many memories that she wanted to shut her eyes and not remember where she was or who was with her. It was impossible to ignore him, though. It was the same make of car, the same sensually masculine being beside her. It was even the same aftershave. It invaded her senses, bringing back feelings as if it were the well-loved perfume of a rose pressed in an album.

'I don't want the place,' Logan rasped. 'I want the man and I've almost got him.'

'You've got him already,' Abigail whispered. 'If you could see him...'

'I have no desire to see him!' Logan ground out. She saw his hands tighten on the wheel and cast a furtive, frightened look at the hard, handsome face. He slanted a look at her like icy lightning and she looked away rapidly, staring down at her tightly clenched fingers.

Logan didn't speak again and Abigail was too shaken and lost even to contemplate conversation. What was there to say to him? His hatred encompassed everything to do with the name Madden. It always had done but she had been too young, too bewitched to know.

'Here we are.' Logan spoke again as the car was gliding to a halt in front of her own offices. This place did not have the splendour of the Steele building and Logan's eyes moved over it with stony indifference as the car stopped.

'Thank you,' Abigail said in little more than a whisper, cringing when his hand came to her arm, his fingers biting into her through the wool of her jacket.

'You'd better harden up, Abigail,' he warned harshly. 'Any other female would have slapped my face and stormed off at this point. But you—you whisper, "Thank you." Your sweetness doesn't get to me any more.'

'It never did,' she said more calmly than she had thought possible. 'You just pretended.' Her wide green eyes looked at him steadily. 'You can take everything from us but you'll not take my character or my belief in people. It was just my misfortune to have met you when I was too young to know better. I'll not judge everyone else by you, though. Somehow, somewhere, I'll start again.'

His hand tightened on her arm but she pulled away and got out of the car, slamming the door and walking towards the building that very soon would be part of Logan's empire. She didn't look round, and long before she got to the steps she heard the Jaguar purr away and move back into the traffic. If she had annoyed him at the end, his driving gave no sign of it. He was, as usual, untouchable, imperious and cold.

'Did you see him?' Martha was waiting as Abigail reached her own floor and went towards her office.

'Yes. I told you not to hope. There was nothing to hope for.'

'I just thought that as you were there for so long—'

'I fainted,' Abigail muttered. 'He brought me back.'

'And?' Martha's face had shown signs of anxiety at the mention of her fainting and Abigail just wanted to get out of here fast.

'And nothing. It was merely a courtesy.'

She walked past and Martha stared after her. She knew all about Logan Steele. She had been at the wedding. Even now, after all that had happened, she couldn't believe that it had all been a sham. They had seemed to be alone even in a crowded church, Abigail so young and beautiful and Logan so powerful and protective. Love had seemed to glow around them like an incredible light. But she had seen Abigail's dreams shattered and now she clenched her hands in rage and went back to her work. What was there to believe in? How did Abigail cope each day?

CHAPTER TWO

WITH her appointments cancelled for the rest of the day, Abigail now had nothing to do. It was useless to work at anything because soon there would be no future at all. Even if she went out of her office and into another part of the building, there would be worried eyes on her, people wondering if she knew anything that they did not. Some of the staff had already taken up other offers and she knew that those who stayed were here through loyalty to her.

The responsibility was like a weight on her heart and yet there was nothing she could do to shield either the staff or her own father. She couldn't even go home yet. If she arrived early he would be in a state of anxiety the moment he saw her car.

She paced about and then went along to make herself a coffee. The long, thickly carpeted corridor was deserted. This was the executive part of the building. Just through the door at the end was the open-plan office where Martha had her desk. At one time this place had almost matched the opulence of the Steele building. It was not as big but it had been a busy, functioning place, the smell of wealth an almost tangible thing in the air.

Now it seemed to be deserted. The office of the vice-chairman was empty. He had left at the first opportunity, left before he could be declared redundant. One day that office was to have been Abigail's but she had leapt temporarily to the office of chairman long before her time, long before her father's retirement and years before she had been ready to make the step.

The boardroom was facing her as she came back and she hurried into her own office after one glance at the name on the door. That room, this corridor was where she had first seen Logan and she didn't want to be reminded. In the quiet she still seemed to hear his voice as she had first heard it. It had been harsh enough, violent enough to stop her in her tracks but she hadn't had time to retreat to the safety of Martha and the busy offices beyond. If she had, he would never have seen her and now she would not be feeling the guilt that refused to go.

Abigail had been nineteen, slender, willowy, with eyes like emeralds and long black hair that curled round her shoulders. She had been working in her father's firm since she had left school the year before. He had always made it plain to her that she would work for him, with him and finally take the firm into her own hands when he retired and Abigail had never thought to defy him. She was sweet-natured, gentle and always willing.

Not that it would have been any easy option to defy Kent Madden. He had fought his way upwards in the business world, a property developer with a keen eye for a good site and a drive to succeed that had brought the Madden Corporation to the top and held it there. Abigail had been supposed to learn everything. Her father had had visions of her being a powerful businesswoman one day with a grasp on the firm and the knowledge that came from starting at the bottom and working up.

That was where she had been at nineteen, at the bottom, and she'd loved the bustle and gossip of the offices, the motherly severity of her father's secretary, Martha Bates. Doing the donkey work had been fun to Abigail and she'd tried not to think of her rather grand and frightening future. It had been many years away. She had been content to type out invoices, make the coffee and cart around heavy business files on demand.

She had been doing that when she had encountered Logan for the first time. He had been thirty-one and alarming, handsome, hard and furious, with more anger in him than she had ever encountered in her life before. It had been in many ways a dramatic meeting, and sheer chance. Minutes later and she would never have seen him, her life would have been completely different. More than that, though, Logan would never have seen her. He would never have known who she was. She would have been safe.

It had been Monday morning, the start of a busy week. The board meeting in the afternoon had been all set up and Abigail had been pushed for time. She had prepared the room under Martha's supervision and now she was taking in the files they would need. There were too many to carry at one go but she was in a hurry. There was still a day's typing on her own desk and she struggled through the heavy swing-door at the end of the corridor with her arms full, the files piled so high that she could barely see over the top of them.

She heard the voice as soon as she opened the door but it was too late to back out; the door had closed behind her and the files were in danger of dropping to the floor.

'Keep looking over your shoulder,' the dark and furious voice threatened, 'because I'll always be there! And I'll get you. Five years! That's how long it will take. Start counting now, and remember—they're inevitable, your fate and my promise!'

The door of her father's office slammed shut, the sound reverberating along the corridor, and Abigail moved instinctively to the wall, well aware that a blind, raging force was bearing down on her. He didn't even see her. He was so inflamed with fury that he simply bumped into her, knocking her shoulder and almost making her lose her balance. There was no chance at all for the files; they cascaded to the floor, scattered like a pack of cards and he didn't even stop.

It was only as he reached the heavy door at the end that it seemed to sink in that he had created a certain amount of chaos. By that time Abigail was on her knees, trying to gather the files into some sort of order and he stopped, looking back and seeing her frantic actions, her slender arms reaching out to set things right. She didn't look round and a curious expression crossed his face for a second. She didn't even look annoyed—no sharp words, not even an irritated glance. She was just picking things up as if he had every right to knock them down.

He walked back and stood looking at her and she looked up then with the most enormous green eyes that he had ever seen.

'I'm sorry,' he offered ruefully. 'I was too damned annoyed to see you.' He crouched down beside her and began to help but she smiled a little warily and shook her head.

'It's all right and you can't help really. They've got to be in order.'

'Alphabetical?'

'No. Priority. I'm afraid they're private,' she added, her face flushing softly, her embarrassment at having to tell him to back off very obvious. He stood and looked down at her, his mouth tilting in an amused way.

'Sorry again in that case.' He nodded at her and began to walk off and Abigail quickly got on with her task, making sure not to look up. He was the most handsome man she had ever seen and she couldn't work out how he could be so furious one minute and then so nice to her. He had smiling grey eyes, like sparkling crystal, an astonishing contrast to his dark hair and tanned face. He looked powerful, full of easy authority and he hadn't gone through the door yet.

She took a stealthy little glance in that direction and he was standing at the door; his hand was on it but he was still watching her.

'What's your name?' His voice had softened and she didn't even consider telling him to mind his own business.

'Abigail. Abigail Madden.'

For a second the grey eyes narrowed, flaring over her from the shining fall of jet-black hair to the slender shape of her beneath the red jumper. Her skirt was dark with matching red flowers and it was spread around her as she knelt. She felt a strange shock as her eyes met the intent gaze. It was a mixture of alarm and an odd pleasure. She looked away hastily, getting back to the files, and he gave a low laugh that shivered its way down her spine.

'Goodbye, Abigail Madden.' She didn't have time to answer because when she looked up he had gone; the door was just swinging shut behind him, and it was a disappointment big enough to bring out a great sigh as she righted the files and got to her feet.

She wondered who he was but she knew that there was not much chance that she would find out. And, oddly enough, she didn't even think about his words as she had come through the door, didn't even wonder why he had been raging at her father. She was too dreamily impressed by the man himself to think further.

It was two days later when she saw him again. She always drove herself to work. Her father said it was the best thing to do—to show everyone that being his daughter brought no special privileges—and in any case she enjoyed the drive and the small feeling of power it gave her that she was working and driving to the office. She had chided herself about her fantasy but it was still there as she left work on Wednesday.

On Wednesdays she stayed in town and went out for a meal with an old friend. Sometimes they went to the cinema later. Her father never worried, however late she was, even when it was winter and dark. He expected her to take care of herself, to be responsible for her own actions.

As she walked out of the building and went to her car her heart almost leapt into her throat when a voice said quietly, 'Hello, Abigail Madden.' When she turned round it was Logan. She couldn't have mistaken that voice in any case but the situation seemed uncanny, as if she was walking in a dream. She hadn't forgotten him for even one minute and he was right there, leaning against a dark-coloured Jaguar, those crystal-grey eyes on her face as she turned.

'Going home?' he asked, his eyes lancing over her, and she was glad that this was the day she went out, because she was dressed in a silky summer suit that was as green as her eyes. She was wearing high heels too. It made her feel sophisticated and he was very sophisticated. The suit he was wearing was superbly tailored and he looked like a prince to Abigail's dazzled eyes. He was very tall, fit and strong—all lithe, muscular power that overwhelmed her.

'Don't you answer when a stranger speaks to you?' he enquired softly. 'If you've been told not to speak to strange men, let me remind you that we've spoken before. I almost knocked you down.'

'I remember.' Abigail's cheeks flushed softly. He had made her feel very young with his remarks about strange men and now she didn't know where to look.

'Can I begin again?' He smiled at her warmly. 'Are you going home?'

'No, I'm going out. This—this is my night when I stay in town.'

'Ah! You've got a date.' For a moment she had the heady feeling that he was disappointed and she quickly corrected him.

'Not a date exactly. I go out with an old schoolfriend on Wednesdays. We go for a meal and then—then sometimes we go to see a film. She's a girl,' Abigail finished in a rush, just to make sure he understood.

'What would she do if you didn't turn up?'

'I always do turn up.' Her heart seemed to take off frighteningly fast and she looked away, biting her lip. 'If for any reason I can't go out then I ring her.'

'Ring her,' Logan ordered quietly.

'But—'

'You're going out with me.' He looked at her steadily and Abigail bit her trembling lips harder, unable to really believe it. He walked closer and stood looking down at her and she managed to find her voice.

'I don't know you,' she whispered, and he nodded in understanding.

'That's why you're going out with me—unless you don't want to know me.'

'I do!' She looked up anxiously, scared that he would change his mind, no thought of danger in her head at all, and Logan smiled into her eyes, his grey eyes slowly inspecting her face with a sort of gentle probing that made her feel weak and strange.

'Then why don't you leave your car here and come with me now? We'll find a telephone and you can ring your friend. Then we'll have dinner. I'll bring you back to your car later.'

Abigail looked up at him like someone in a trance and he touched her flushed cheek lightly.

'There's nothing to be afraid of. All right?' He was so wonderfully reassuring and Abigail nodded. There *was* something to be afraid of. She should have been very much afraid of this man with the soft, dark voice and the startling grey eyes but she was too bewitched to know it. He had soothed his way into her soul.

The phone rang and Abigail came back to reality with a start.

'Brian Wingate on the line for you,' Martha said and put her straight through before she had time to come out of the world of dreams and back into the bleak and frightening present.

'How are things?' He sounded safe and comfortable and Abigail smiled as she answered.

'Hanging by a thread. I expect the thread to snap at any moment.'

'Well, there's no new word about,' he assured her steadily. 'What do you do, Abigail? Do you wait for the axe to fall or do you slide out from under now?'

'I can't slide out from under, Brian,' she pointed out wearily. 'I'm the one they have to throw the book at. I have to see this out—Madden's last stand.'

'You're not the one,' he said forcefully. 'The only reason you're there in that position is because your father is ill. Are you telling me that if Martha Bates had been forced to hold the fort she would have had to make a last stand?'

'Knowing Martha,' Abigail mused, 'she probably would have done. In any case,' she added more firmly, 'I have the name. I'm a Madden. I can't just hide.'

'You're merely a girl!'

'I'm twenty-four and I feel eighty. The girl disappeared—somewhere.'

He swore under his breath and for a moment she thought that he had simply decided to say nothing more; then he said, 'Look, love, I'm flying to Germany in the morning. I may be a week or even longer. Let me fix you up with us before I go.'

'No, thanks, Brian. I have to stick this out to the end. I appreciate—'

'You're not expected to appreciate anything. I can use you in the firm. You're good. The trouble with you, Abigail, is that you're too good, too gentle.' She bit down on her lip. That's more or less what Logan had said this morning but he had said it much more coldly. 'When I get back,' Brian went on, 'I'll phone immediately. In the meantime...'

'I'll keep my back to the wall and my finger on the trigger,' she assured him, forcing a bright laugh.

'Dear, unworldly Abigail,' he mourned quietly. 'Nothing stops a wolf—not this wolf. Logan Steele is power beyond imagining. You know that.' He sighed deeply. 'I won't even be here to offer a shoulder to cry on. Take care.'

'I will.' She put the phone down and smiled ruefully. She might need a shoulder to cry on but it would not be Brian's. It would never be anyone's. Since Logan she hadn't wanted any man to care for her. It was too dangerous, too cruel and not fair. She still dreamed of Logan and woke up bewildered. It had been too wonderful to be true in the first place, too cruel to be real when it had ended.

When she finally got home, the usual words were spoken.

'Anything new?'

'Nothing.' She was not about to tell him about her visit to Logan's office. It would have driven him over the edge. He had always hated Logan. As she had cancelled any appointments, there was nothing at all to discuss, and once again Abigail was alone.

Kent Madden was almost completely silent throughout dinner, merely grunting his thanks when their long-time housekeeper, Rose, served the meal. She knew, of course—everyone knew—and she cast a worried eye at Abigail's pale face every time she came into the room. Even Rose was relying on her, expecting miracles, and it all weighed heavily on Abigail, even at home.

There was nowhere to run, nowhere to go. It was utterly frustrating to be so vulnerable and helpless.

'Something has got to be done!' her father suddenly grated as they were having coffee. 'There must be some action we can take, something that I'm missing.' He got up and paced about, once again working himself up. 'It's never been a problem to get hold of money.'

'No amount of money would match the Steele Group,' Abigail pointed out quietly. 'Even without the backing of two powerful banks Logan has millions of his own.'

'And you're entitled to some of that!' Kent Madden spun round and looked at her fiercely. 'You never divorced him. If you had he would have had to part with plenty.'

'I doubt it. In any case, I want nothing from Logan. I wouldn't accept a crust.'

'You're too soft,' he said scathingly. 'One day, my girl, you'll learn that you have to grab the things you want. You've let him off scot-free!'

'I was just glad to survive,' Abigail murmured. They had been through this before and the subject was painful and distasteful. When she had walked out on Logan she had left that life completely behind and she did not need to be reminded of it.

Her father sank into his usual silence and she made her way to bed before he could start up again. He always made her feel that somehow this was all her fault, that if she had never married Logan all this would never have happened. It would have, though. She was not nineteen now and the memory of Logan's threat of that day five years ago was all too real. Even when he had been married to her, even when she had been in his arms, he had been planning her father's destruction.

She lay in bed, too het up to sleep, and her mind went back to Logan. How cold and heartless he had seemed today—just power with no drop of humanity in him. He would continue to tear them apart until they were finished. He might feel that the Madden Corporation was still viable but it was not viable for them. With Logan's wealth and backing it was perhaps possible to save it. What did he intend to do? Would he swoop down on them and take over or would he let them sink away into oblivion?

His face swam into her mind, first hard and cold and then warm and gentle as it had once seemed to be. How could she have been so trusting, so naïve? From the first she had been under his spell and, looking back, she could see that she had been eager to believe anything, just to be with him.

After that first evening Logan had called her every day, but never at home; in fact she'd thought he had no idea where she lived. He'd wanted her to go out with him constantly and Abigail had taken to staying in town in the evenings to be with him. Her father had made no comment. He hadn't known about Logan and she hadn't told him. He had, as usual, been wrapped up in his own schemes, his own plans and, provided that she was at work each day, he'd paid no attention to her at all.

He had always been like that. Without friends she would have been lonely. She had had no mother by then and her father had discussed nothing but business. The fact that more often than not she was late in at night had been no concern of his. He'd simply assumed that she was with friends and Abigail had not enlightened him because, deep down, she'd known that he would explode with rage.

She'd never thought of the way she had first met Logan, of the dark certainty of the threat, but there was enough memory of it at the back of her mind to make her keep her own counsel. Meanwhile she was ensnared, drowning in the silver-grey of Logan's eyes, bewitched by his smile.

At the weekends she was out all day with Logan, walking, driving, going to the theatre and eating out. Sometimes they ate at little country places, sometimes in rather exclusive restaurants where Abigail would have been intimidated had it not been for the sight of him across the table from her, the way he took her hand to lead her to her chair.

He was treating her carefully and she knew it. She was utterly enthralled by him but he never let her get too close. Sometimes when she left him she felt frustrated, longing for something she barely understood, longing for just one moment of commitment, one kiss, but Logan never did more than hold her hand and smile into her eyes. She was completely safe with him and completely bewildered by his actions.

He didn't seem to be able to keep away from her for more than a day and yet he never pressed any advantage and Abigail wished he would. She longed to be swept off her feet, to dive headlong into the swirling attraction she felt for him.

One weekend they met at a restaurant and for the first time there was dancing. It scared her a little to see the other people moving round the floor, and the thought of being in Logan's arms if he should ask her to dance made her tremble. She had wanted to be in his arms since she had first seen him but contrarily, now that the opportunity was near, she felt too shaken to contemplate it.

'Come and dance with me.' Logan stood as they finished their meal and looked across at her, his smiling eyes holding her fast.

Tingles ran down her spine and her legs would scarcely hold her up as she rose. He came to her, his arm coming round her waist as he led her to the floor, and as he touched her awareness shot through her like a flame. She wasn't even thinking at all as he turned her in his arms and began to move with her to the slow, sensuous rhythm of the dance.

Their bodies touched for the first time and everything inside her flared more as she felt the tightly leashed-in strength of him against her softness. Beneath her hand his shoulder tensed, his powerful muscles moving beneath the smooth cloth of his jacket. She looked up into his face but he was looking beyond her, unsmiling, his face taut with something almost like anger, and she saw again the command he had, the control he had of his own mind and body. There was a dominance and mastery about him that left her feeling awestricken.

He looked down at her, his gaze moving slowly over her upturned face, searching every feature, his strange, silvery eyes glowing like the eyes of some beautiful hunting creature, and then he smiled, his hand lifting to caress her cheek in a tender gesture that seemed to be torn from him.

'Abigail,' he said softly. 'Beautiful Abigail with hair like a blackbird's wing and eyes like emeralds.'

She didn't blush at such softly spoken words although normally she would have been utterly confused. Instead, something sweet and exciting burst inside her, curling around, flooding her whole body with delight. Her breath seemed to have left her and she tried to regain it with a shaken sigh. His eyes narrowed on her and he took one trembling hand in his, bringing it to his chest and holding it there against the steady beat of his heart.

Neither of them was smiling now. They seemed to be incapable of looking away from each other, until Logan brought her closer, his face against her hair.

'Shall we go?' he asked quietly, and all Abigail could do was nod. Words were beyond her. Something had happened to her that had never happened before. Every nerve-ending was tingling, her heartbeats threatened to choke her, and as she walked from the floor and left the restaurant with Logan's arm around her waist she shivered with reaction.

He took her hand, walking beside her to his car with the same smooth animal grace she had been noticing since she had first seen him. He was miles beyond her reach, light years above her, and tears came into her eyes, hot and burning. It wasn't fair. There would never be anyone like Logan again, ever. He would tire of seeing her. What could he possibly want with an immature nineteen-year-old? There must be women lining up to go out with him—hundreds of women.

In the car, Logan turned to look at her and she quickly looked away, hiding her face, afraid that he would see the stupid tears that hadn't left her shining eyes. He tilted her small chin and turned her to face him and when she refused to look at him his lips brushed hers softly as he leaned across to her.

It was gentle, experimental, hardly a kiss at all, but she gasped with the shock of it, trembling violently, and he brought her towards him, his lips teasing the side of her mouth before he pulled her fully into his arms and kissed her deeply. His lips were hard, warm, instantly insistent and his whole body tensed with shock as he felt her response. It was inevitable, unavoidable. Pure sexual pleasure raced through Abigail for the first time in her life and Logan gathered her closer, his arms imprisoning her as she tilted her face willingly and innocently.

The kiss seemed to go on for ages but actually it was no more than a few seconds and then Logan drew away, releasing her and sitting back, his eyes closed as he fought to control the breathing that was ragged in his throat. Abigail was shaking uncontrollably and he looked across at her, taking her hand and squeezing it in his almost cruelly.

'I'll take you home,' he offered thickly, but she shook her head.

'I—I have my car.'

'You're not fit to drive, Abigail. I'll take you.'

'It's a long way and—and, in any case, if my car is here then I'll not be able . . . Tomorrow is Sunday . . . If you want to see me—'

'You know I want to see you,' he told her huskily. 'You'll come on the train. I'll be waiting for you at the station. Ten o'clock. We'll have the whole day.'

'I'll tell you where I live,' she began, delirious with joy that he still wanted to see her even after he had kissed her, but Logan simply started the car and didn't look at her.

'I know where you live.' She didn't question that. Logan knew everything. He was perfection. She worshipped him.

At her door he didn't kiss her again and Abigail was glad. If he had done she would not have been able to make her legs walk inside.

'Tomorrow, early,' he ordered as he lifted her hand to his lips. 'I'll be waiting, Abigail.'

She couldn't sleep. It was all like a dream. Her father had still been in his study and she had simply popped her head round the door and said goodnight, thankful that it had not dawned on him that a car had pulled away from the house, that it had obviously not been hers. He hardly glanced at her but she didn't care. Her heart and mind were singing—Logan, Logan. Tomorrow she would see him again and this time it would be different.

He was waiting as she got off the train the next day and his face lit up at the sight of her. His glance flared over her and she knew that she looked nice. Her summer skirt was dark green, the same colour as the sleeveless blouse she wore, and her tiny waist was encircled by a golden belt to make it more dressed up. She wore high-heeled gold sandals and Logan laughed as his eyes moved over her slender legs and saw her foot gear.

'I see we're not walking,' he murmured in amusement, and Abigail found it possible to laugh too, for the first time feeling almost an equal.

She dived into her shoulder bag and brought out flat sandals, dangling them in front of him.

'I'm prepared for anything,' she pronounced gaily.

'Are you?' He looked at her steadily for a second and her face flushed softly before he took pity on her and held out his hand. 'Let's go,' he ordered quietly. 'I suppose I'll have to get you in early tonight. Tomorrow is a work day. We'll start now so as not to miss a minute.'

It was exhilarating and she snuggled into his car, turning to him eagerly.

'Where are we going?' She looked so bright-eyed, so beguiling that Logan stared at her for a second before answering.

'On the river. I've got a boat moored by a small inn not too many miles away. We'll go there and eat and then we'll sail away into the distance.'

Abigail could have hugged herself with excitement and he glanced at her, his mouth twisting in amusement.

'I don't expect you've been on a boat before.'

'Not on the Thames,' she agreed. She tossed her head proudly. 'I've been on a cruise, though. I've been to Jamaica and cruised round the Caribbean.'

'Oh! Big stuff,' he mocked softly. 'There's nothing so exciting to offer here. There may be the odd duck but nothing to contend with such sophistication.'

'You—' Abigail pouted '—are laughing at me.'

'It seems to be a good idea,' he confessed quietly. 'You look like an enchanted princess. Laughter is a very safe emotion. I think we'll laugh all day.'

That succeeded in wiping any amusement from Abigail's face because she knew what he meant. He had devoured her with his eyes as she had stepped off the train and now there was an atmosphere crackling between them, frightening and thrilling. She wanted him to touch her again; she wanted it so badly that her heart began to beat with a new cadence, and he knew. It was there in the stillness of his face, in the tight grip he had on the wheel.

'I'm sorry,' she whispered.

'Can you help it?' he asked darkly, not even pretending that he didn't know what she meant.

'No.' She couldn't help it. She wanted Logan to love her, to make love to her. She had felt like that for days and it was hurting.

'Neither can I,' he confessed quietly. 'Maybe this should be our last outing.'

His words were so unexpected that Abigail caught her breath, her flushed cheeks going white.

'Don't leave me, Logan,' she whispered despairingly. His head shot round and as he saw the pallor of her face he pulled into the side of the busy road, reaching for her and crushing her against him.

'God! I can't!' he muttered hoarsely. His head bent and his lips caught hers almost violently, the intensity of the kiss sending liquid fire through her veins, and instantly her lips parted beneath his, her innocent surrender making him tighten his grip for a second.

'Not here,' he said huskily, putting her away from him with thrilling reluctance.

It was only as she looked up with bewildered eyes that she saw several astonished bystanders, and by that time Logan's Jaguar was smoothly moving, saving her embarrassment.

'Oh, dear,' she murmured, and Logan threw his head back, laughing delightedly, the tension easing from his shoulders.

'Well, they didn't bend down to look more closely,' he pointed out with a grin. His silver glance lanced through her. 'Do you still want to go on that boat trip?' he asked softly.

'Yes.' He was asking her if he had frightened her and she knew she should be wary but she loved him too much for that. She had never felt like this before and Logan felt like it too. Nothing else mattered.

CHAPTER THREE

IT WAS a wonderful day. They went to look at the boat that was moored by the old inn and Abigail took off her sandals and climbed on board, eagerly inspecting everything. It was not a grand boat but it was much bigger than she had expected. It was rocking slightly on the sunlit water and she stood on the deck and breathed in the warm, honey-scented air.

'It's marvellous!' she proclaimed, and Logan looked at her ruefully, his eyes making a lightning foray over her entranced face.

'You're the easiest girl in the world to please, Abigail,' he assured her in amusement as he leapt down to the river bank.

She lost some of her animation then, thinking that she detected a note of cynicism. She felt embarrassed, as if she was behaving like a child, and the smile died on her face.

'I suppose you're used to more sophisticated women,' she managed sharply, stifling the hurt that rose at once. It felt as if he had rejected her, been bored with her enthusiasm, and for a minute she was close to tears.

'Very sophisticated women,' he mocked, his grey eyes inspecting her flushed face as he looked up at her. 'They never show enthusiasm. This little boat would bore them senseless.'

Abigail's soft mouth drooped and she looked away from the taunting crystal eyes, the day suddenly losing its glow.

'I can't pretend,' she confessed in a choked voice. 'If I like something, I have to show it. Perhaps, one day, I'll be able to curb my childish excitement.'

'Come here, Abigail.' The low, dark voice sent a shiver down her spine. It seemed to reach right into the centre of her being and her wide green eyes met his unhappily. 'Collect your sandals and come here,' he ordered softly, and she picked up her sandals and stepped to the edge of the boat.

He reached for her, his hands spanning her tiny waist as he lifted her down, and it was done so gently that Abigail felt pleasure run all through her. When she bent to fasten her sandals, Logan held her arm, and as she straightened up his hands cupped her flushed face and held it up to his.

'You're beautiful,' he said softly. His hands swept back her hair, his glance running over the black, shining strands. 'You're the sweetest girl in all the world and if you were sophisticated *I* would be bored senseless.'

He watched her for a minute, seeing the hurt die away, and Abigail was unable to speak. Her heart was pounding at the look in his eyes and he bent his head to hers, his cool lips brushing lightly over her mouth.

'Let's eat,' he said quietly as he lifted his head. He was unsmiling, unnaturally still and the same feeling was surging between them that had been there before in the car. He just turned her towards the inn, his arm coming possessively round her waist, and Abigail held herself stiffly, scared that she would turn to him and wind her arms around him. Her feelings were too strong to be controlled and all she could do was pretend not to be there at all.

'Don't be afraid of me, Abigail,' he murmured gently, turning her towards him.

'I'm not,' she managed, even though it was not really the truth.

'I'll never let anything hurt you,' he said, his breath warm against her cheek as he pulled her closer. 'You're precious. I need to care for you. You can come to me with no fear.'

His hand moved from her waist to touch her neck, his fingers gently caressing, and Abigail gave in, resting against him as they walked, her arm sliding around his waist, joy bursting inside her when he held her tightly against him.

During the meal Logan managed to put her at her ease and by the time they took the boat out she felt safe enough to show her enchantment with everything. They moved slowly down the Thames, always in quiet, sunlit waters, and she looked at the houses by the river, some of them huge and impressive, their gardens running down to the water's edge. It seemed like paradise and by the time they were cruising back to the mooring Abigail was tired and deliriously happy.

Logan had been gentle all day. They had sat on deck drinking lemonade and talking all the time. Her skin was softly touched by the sun and the dying rays caught the brilliant green glow of her eyes.

'We'll tie up and then clear our things away,' Logan announced as they touched the bank. 'After that, it's home fast for you.'

Abigail went into the little cabin to clear away but the glow had died. She didn't want to leave Logan. Every time she left him and went back home it got harder and harder to say goodnight. When he jumped back on board she was standing in the cabin just staring at nothing.

'What is it?' He came up behind her quietly and Abigail hung her head, biting miserably at her lip.

'I—I don't want to go,' she whispered. 'I don't want to leave you.'

'You're nineteen,' Logan reminded her, 'not one of my many sophisticated women.'

'Don't!' She turned to him, her eyes filling with pain, and he swore softly under his breath as he caught her in his arms.

'There are no sophisticated women,' he muttered unevenly. 'If there were, do you think I would look at any of them when you were there? I'm trying to keep this light, trying to protect you.' When she just went on looking at him with swimming green eyes he pulled her closer almost roughly, his fingers tangling in her shining hair. 'Dear God, Abbie!' he said hoarsely. 'I want you and you know it!'

He began to kiss her—hard, fast, hungry kisses that parted her lips and sent burning feelings through her body. She swayed towards him, winding her arms around his waist, and he pulled her head to his shoulder as she lifted her face, desperate for his lips.

Logan's hand swept over her, caressing every curve, melting her inside, and she found her legs giving way, making her sink down, trying to take him with her.

'No!' he gasped unevenly. 'Let's get out of here.' His voice was shaken but he kept his arm around her as if he could no more endure being parted than she could, and as they left the boat and walked along the bank Abigail was still shaking with the intensity of feeling that had swept over them. It was dark by now, the light almost gone, and she was glad that the darkness hid her hot face.

'In here,' Logan said almost harshly. 'You need a drink and so do I.'

He pushed the door of the inn open and they were instantly surrounded by noise. There was music from some hidden speakers, laughter, loud conversation, and the small room was dimly lit and crowded.

'Just what we need,' he muttered. Most people were at the bar and he found a small, darkened corner where the red-covered benches almost hid them from sight. 'Sit here,' he ordered. 'I'll get our drinks.'

She was glad to sink to the seat. Her trembling had by no means stopped and she was glad, too, for the brief time by herself as Logan went to the bar. She had always faced things. She had never been allowed to do otherwise and she faced this squarely now. She was in love with Logan. She wanted him as much as he wanted her. It was frightening and thrilling, something she had never known, but she knew that she wanted to be with him for the rest of her life. If he didn't feel the same she didn't know what she would do.

He came back and slid in beside her, handing her a brandy.

'Drink it. Dutch courage,' he murmured ironically, and Abigail tried to sip the fiery liquid. It made her choke and she felt once again unspeakably young, far distant from Logan. Her hands trembled on the table-top and she looked down at them in despair, almost jumping when one of Logan's strong hands covered both hers.

'Sweet, sweet Abbie,' he whispered. He leaned forward, his lips tracing her tender jawline, and then with a groan he put his drink down and moved closer, his arm coming round her shoulders. 'I give in,' he breathed. His wrist tilted her chin and as she looked into his burning eyes his mouth closed over her own in urgent possession.

Nothing could have stopped her kissing him back. Her head was against his shoulder, her lips parted in surrender, and Logan's mouth covered hers with masterful tenderness. She forgot the dimly lit room, the many people, and once again it was Logan who stopped.

'We have to go,' he breathed, his lips tracing her hot cheeks. 'We seem to choose the damnedest places.'

He took her hand, helping her out from the bench, and then they were walking from the place, Logan lifting her hand to his lips as they went back to his car. In the dark privacy of the Jaguar he pulled her to him, his hand smoothing her hair and then cupping her cheek.

'What would you say if I asked you to come back to my flat with me?' he asked huskily, looking deeply into her eyes. In the light from the inn she could see the tautness of his face, the almost rueful twist to his mouth. And she had no doubt at all about what he meant.

'I would say yes,' she whispered. 'I love you, Logan. I don't want to be anywhere except with you.'

'Why are you so sweet, so beautiful?' he groaned against her hair. He looked down at her and kissed her very gently. 'I never want to let you out of my sight,' he murmured against her lips. 'Every time we're together I try to be sensible but parting from you is agonising. Don't leave me ever again, Abigail.'

'I won't,' she whispered. He put her gently away and started the car and Abigail rested her head against his shoulder. She had wanted to go with Logan the first time she had seen him. She had wanted to run to him and be swept up into his arms. It was no shock. It was fate— her fate—and she would stay with him as long as he wanted her. No thought of home, or her father entered her mind. She was where she was meant to be— with Logan.

*   *   *

In his flat she was impressed by the taste and luxury and she looked around with wide-eyed interest.

'Can I explore?' She didn't look at him because now that they were here she just could not believe it. She was slightly afraid too—afraid of the unknown.

'No,' he said quietly. 'You can explore later.' He took her into his arms, turning her towards him. 'Don't be afraid of me. I want you, my sweet darling, and I would never hurt you.'

The way he was looking at her was heavenly and Abigail melted in his arms. She believed him. Logan would never hurt her.

'Don't ever send me away,' she whispered, looking up into his eyes, and he swept her up against the hard wall of his chest, holding her tightly as he walked to the bedroom.

'Never in my whole life,' he promised thickly. 'I couldn't exist if you were not beside me.'

He undressed her gently and slowly and Abigail watched with dazed eyes as Logan undressed. She had never seen a man naked before and his burning eyes never left her as he drank in the sight of her loveliness. Her black hair was spread across the pillow, her silken limbs a temptation that brought flaring desire to his face.

When he came to her and drew her close, Abigail gave a sigh of contentment and Logan looked down at her.

'What?' he murmured, and she smiled, a siren look of enchantment about her face.

'I just belong here,' she whispered. 'It's as if I've always been waiting, and now I know what for.'

'Abbie!' His lips closed over hers with fierce demand— an explosive kiss that made her cling to him, trembling. He caressed every part of her, his lips following the path of his urgent hands as Abigail twisted beneath him, whispering his name in a voice she hardly recognised.

Her hands traced his skin, twisted in his dark hair, and when he finally moved to possess her she gave a small, sobbing cry, her limbs parting to accept him. His eyes burned down at her, locking with her green gaze.

'You're mine!' His face tightened with urgent passion. 'You belong to me. For ever, from this moment on.'

'For ever.' Abigail closed her eyes, arching against him, and she believed it. Being with Logan was her life. She knew that. She had known it for days and days. She couldn't think beyond it.

It was only the next day that the world had to be faced, and reality—the reality of her father. Logan insisted on taking her home early, before anyone had time to leave for work.

'He's not going to like this,' Abigail pointed out worriedly, and Logan caught her to him, looking down at her seriously.

'He has no choice at all. You and I are going to be married. Nothing and nobody can stop that. Like it or not, your father has to face it.'

Though it was a little worrying, Abigail was too dreamy with happiness to resist when Logan put her into his car and drove her home in the early morning. She expected sharp words from her father and even a slight amount of unpleasantness but she didn't anticipate the scene that would occur when Logan and her father faced each other.

Since she had first seen him, she had been so wrapped up in her feelings for Logan that any sort of common sense seemed to have fled. Now everything she had to face was like a cold dash of water. Now she had to stand

between two battling giants with hatred sparkling in the
air like white heat.

Her father was just leaving his study as she came into
the hall with Logan following and he seemed to freeze
at the sight of them. Kent Madden didn't even look at
Abigail. It didn't seem to dawn on him that his daughter
had been out all night. She was unimportant. All that
mattered was the hatred.

'Get out of my house!' Abigail hardly recognised her
father's voice as he ground out the words at Logan.

'Daddy!' Abigail tried to intervene but he ignored her.

'Get out!' he repeated savagely. His eyes seemed to
focus slowly on Abigail and he frowned. 'Where the hell
have you been?' he snarled.

'She's with me,' Logan said curtly. 'We can work this
out in a civilised manner or any way you want, but
Abigail is with me.'

The announcement brought even more rage to her
father's face and he reached out to take her arm.

'Go to your room! I'll deal with this,' he snapped,
but Logan's arm swept round her, pulling her to the
shelter of his shoulder, tucking her close and holding her
tightly.

'Abigail goes with me!'

Logan's final words seemed at last to penetrate through
her father's rage. He looked at them both and it dawned
on him just what was happening.

'So this is how you intend to do it. You think you can
get at me through Abigail. It's not a good move, Steele.
My daughter doesn't control anything at all yet. You'll
get nothing there.'

'All I want is Abigail,' Logan stated coldly. 'She
doesn't even need her clothes from this house. Anything
she wants I'll get for her.'

'She's nineteen!' Her father's face became bright with anger and Abigail made a move to go to him, to stop this terrifying battle but Logan's arm held her fast.

'Old enough to know her own mind,' he pointed out with equal coldness. 'Old enough to marry me. You can come to the wedding. You can give her your blessing. It's up to you.'

'You'll get no blessing from me!' Kent Madden shouted hoarsely, and Logan turned away, taking Abigail with him.

'*I* want nothing from you,' he reminded her father icily. 'Nothing you can give. What I will finally have from you I'll take! Abigail is nobody's property. She's outside all this. We simply came to tell you that we're getting married.'

They were at the door and her father hadn't even moved a step. Abigail looked at him miserably, regret in her eyes. She had never had any say in anything at all. Mostly her father ignored her unless it was about work and now she was just an object to be fought over.

Obviously her father mistook her glance because a spasm of triumph crossed his face.

'Stay here, Abigail,' he said more calmly. 'You don't know Steele. He's ruthless, cruel!' He didn't say he loved her. He didn't even bother to remind her that he was her father.

'I have to go with Logan,' she murmured sadly. 'I want to go with him. I love him. Why does it have to be like this?'

'She'll not marry you!' Kent Madden raised his voice again, ignoring her, and Logan glanced at him with contempt.

'She's mine already and she'll stay mine. This is permanent. My secretary will send you the wedding arrangements. Come or stay away as you please, but if you let her down,' he added, his voice lowered in menace, 'if you're not there to give her away like any other father with his daughter it will be just one more count against you. I'll not forget it.'

There was something in his voice that Abigail had never heard before. For a moment, Logan was another person but she didn't have the chance to think about it. She was outside the house and in Logan's car, her past left behind. Her father didn't attempt to follow. He didn't even come to the door. And in Logan's arms there was a comfort she had never had in her life.

Her father had come to the wedding after all. He had given her away and he'd made a great effort to be normal, though he hadn't spoken to Logan or any of the guests on Logan's side of the church. She had told herself that it was because he loved her too much to let her down but now she knew differently. Even then, even before Logan had really started his deadly vendetta, Kent Madden had feared him.

Abigail sighed and turned on her side, desperately seeking sleep. It was the only way she had of escaping, and even then she often woke up in the middle of the night, reaching out for Logan and then remembering that he was not there and never would be there again.

It had not been a good idea to see him today. No good would come of it, no help for them. All that had happened had been a stirring-up of the bitterness and she had shown herself to be as vulnerable as ever. Her fainting spell must have angered Logan and it had left her feeling very foolish. It would have been a good idea to lie low and not remind him of her existence while he went on his deadly way as he had done all this time.

Next morning, the expected summons to the bank did not come and the day was spent in waiting. For once, nobody was pestering her. Her phone hardly rang at all and by the time she was ready to leave for home Abigail was more worried than ever. No news might be good news but this was unnerving. Martha met her gaze with puzzled eyes as she left the office.

'What's happening?' She looked at Abigail a little anxiously.

'Something dreadful, I expect.' Abigail stood by Martha's desk and sighed loudly. 'They're probably all closeted somewhere making a great plan to sink us swiftly.'

'Never say die,' Martha urged, but Abigail shrugged wearily.

'What else is there to say? Today nothing happened but we all know that it *will* happen. Maybe tomorrow.'

Certainly tomorrow, she thought as she left the building. Perhaps by next week there would be no need to come here every day. By next week this whole place might very well belong to Logan.

It couldn't come soon enough. She was tired, worn out. When it was over she would not have to think about Logan again. All this time, throughout all the fight, she had held him at the back of her mind. When it was finally over she would be free and she would just go away. She would probably take a job with Brian.

Martha caught up with her just before she got to her car.

'Let's go for a coffee.' She planted herself beside Abigail and ignored any surprised looks.

'All right.' Abigail turned back. Why not? When she got home there would be the usual questions and the usual recriminations. At the moment she preferred

Martha's company. Being late back was no problem and although Martha's attitude was unexpected Abigail was grateful for the break in routine.

'I never expected all this, you know,' Martha confided when they were settled at a corner table of a busy little café nearby. 'Well, not after you married Logan, anyway.'

'I can't think why,' Abigail stated glumly. 'I was nothing, after all. I still don't know what it's all about really. Battles in business I can understand, but this enmity, this bitterness! Daddy was furious about the wedding but this is all Logan's doing. There was something going on before I even met Logan but he never would tell me, neither would my father. In fact, after I married Logan I didn't see my father much. It was too traumatic. He just used to fire questions at me—questions I couldn't answer.'

'Your father ruined the firm that Logan's father set up,' Martha informed her quietly. 'As far as I know, it was all straightforward business.' She shrugged ruefully. 'Some survive, some go under. Logan's father went under; in fact, he died.'

'But that wasn't my father's fault!' Abigail protested.

'I've told you all I know.' Martha looked at her steadily. 'If I knew any more, I would tell you. You're the one who is suffering and it was all before your time.'

'I played right into Logan's hands,' Abigail mused with a far-away look on her face.

Martha frowned grimly before saying, 'He loved you.'

'Oh, please!' Abigail gave a shaken laugh. 'What is this, Martha? I'm not a child and I'm not an idiot. Logan used me to get at my father. He wouldn't even let me have a baby because he knew it wasn't going to last as a marriage. I was just a means to an end.'

'Suppose you're wrong?' Martha asked softly.

'He needed me as a weapon. You must have heard all the talk about Fenella Mitchell. She was before my time, during my time and I expect she's with Logan still.'

Abigail's face tightened at the thought of the beautiful woman who had never really been out of Logan's life. She was supposed to be his solicitor but she was much more than that. Everybody had known, and finally Abigail had known too. Logan had not even bothered to deny it in the end. She had left him for a lot of reasons but Fenella Mitchell had been the main reason. It was easy now to look back coldly and admit it.

Logan had always been wealthy. His father's firm might have been ruined but Logan had money of his own—money that had come from his grandfather and uncle in America. He had used that to rebuild the firm. He had also used it to crush her father.

'I'll have to go.' Abigail stood to leave and Martha sighed. Her attempt to mediate had been useless. The whole thing was a tangle that would never unwind.

'Not done a lot of good, have I?' she asked woefully, and Abigail managed to summon up a smile.

'It would take a miracle.' And there were no miracles. According to her father, Logan had the monopoly of those and he kept them for himself.

When she got home, the coldness of the house hit her afresh. It had always been like this, for as long as she could remember. Her mother was just a hazy dream at the back of her mind but she knew that even before her mother's death her father had been totally absorbed in his business interests and nothing else.

'I'm back, Rose.' She popped her head round the kitchen door and found Rose busily preparing dinner.

'I'll not be long,' Rose said comfortably. 'You're a bit late tonight but it's only what I expected. Anyway, you're safely in. Your father's in his study, I think.'

He would be, Abigail mused. Going in there was unavoidable, too. He expected a run-down on the day's events even when there was nothing to report. She stiffened her spine and walked across the hall, opening the door of the study quietly.

At first, she thought he was not in the room and she called out to him but got no answer at all. Abigail was just about to leave when she saw him. He was lying on the floor behind his desk. She could see his feet and when she ran round she could tell at once that he had collapsed with no warning, had fallen before he could alert Rose.

She dropped to her knees beside him, her hand coming to touch his face, and it was cold, moist with sweat. His breathing was erratic, laboured and Abigail knew that what she had dreaded for weeks had at last happened. It was his heart and she raced from the room, calling to Rose and then getting to the telephone to call an ambulance. It might be too late. She just didn't know, but he was so cold—icily cold—his lips blue.

Later it seemed to Abigail that she had lived a whole week during the following hour. Rose had been no help at all. Panic had been her reaction as usual but the men had arrived with the ambulance more quickly than Abigail had expected. Even so, things looked bad. Her father had come round on the way to the hospital but he had not really been aware of his surroundings, not really aware of her.

'You should have someone with you,' the sister at the hospital said now, and Abigail phoned Martha. There was no one else. She might have phoned Brian but she knew he was in Germany, and even Martha was out. Abigail left a message on her answering machine and then settled down to wait by herself, to pace about and worry.

Once again she had not eaten. She was shaking, cold in spite of the warmth of the hospital. It seemed like the final blow, the last fierce lash of destiny, aimed at her. She had little hope because hope had gone a long time ago. Now everything had gone wrong and once again Abigail blamed herself, going over and over in her mind the things she had done or not done these past few weeks, searching for some way she could have avoided this.

'Sit down!' A strong hand took her arm, propelling her to a seat, the sound of the voice sending colder shivers down her spine.

'What are you doing here? How did you...?'

'Martha Bates phoned me,' Logan said shortly, his hand still forcing her to sit. 'You left a message on her answering machine and she rang me.' He watched Abigail grimly. 'Apparently I should have anticipated this. She more or less ordered me to rescue you. I've been roundly condemned and sentenced without a trial by that staunch ally of yours.'

'I never asked her to phone you,' Abigail protested unevenly. 'I phoned her because I had—had no one else and—'

'Damn you, Abigail! You're my wife!' Logan sat beside her and stared at her ferociously. 'Who else would you call but me?'

'Please!' Abigail began to laugh—a high, shaken laugh that showed how close to collapse she was herself. 'You're the last person I would want, the last person to come to my rescue at any time, and this is my *father*! Did you come to see the final act?'

Logan snarled something beneath his breath, stood
and walked away from her and she watched him with
panic-stricken eyes. He was just going to leave and she
did need him here. She hadn't meant to say those things
because it was not Logan who had brought this heart
attack on. It was her father's own attitude to everything,
the way he drank, the way he drove himself and
everybody else. Whatever Logan had done it was not
this.

Her eyes closed with sheer weariness and she sat with
her head bowed, jumping nervously when Logan grasped
her arm and pulled her to her feet, unable to believe that
he had come back.

'Come with me,' he ordered grimly. 'You need something inside you and you need to be warm.'

'I can't leave...'

'You can. Just round the corner is a small place where
we can eat and get a drink. I've asked the staff and they
say it will be some time before there's any change in the
situation. I'm taking my mobile phone with me and
they'll ring if anything happens. No good can come of
sitting here worrying. In any case, I'll not allow it. You're
coming with me.'

It was useless to protest with Logan. His determination had always taken her along with anything he
wanted and nothing was different now. In any case, it
was only sound common sense and Abigail knew it.

'I'll come,' she sighed, and he shot one of his lightning,
crystal glances in her direction.

'There was never any doubt about that,' he grunted
irritably.

Hunger, shock and the sheer misery of the past few
months had left Abigail almost numb and now that she
was with Logan she realised it. She was not fit to cope

with anything, neither a dying business nor the fact that her father was probably dying too. She just sat and stared across at Logan as he ordered their drinks and food from the bar of the small dark place he had found close to the hospital.

It was almost empty at this hour. Most of the chairs had been stacked ready for closing time and she looked at her watch with surprise. Almost ten. She had been at the hospital for a long time without even knowing it. There would be hours before any news came from the unit where her father was fighting for his life.

Would he fight? Once, she would have been certain of his battle but now she was not too sure. He seemed to have been crumbling before her eyes for a long time and she had done nothing about it.

'I knew this was coming. I should have acted,' she muttered to herself.

'What?' Logan had come back without her even knowing it and she glanced up at him with dazed eyes.

'I was thinking aloud,' she confessed, and when he went on staring at her in his devastating manner she dropped her head and continued, 'I should have seen this coming. I *did* see it coming but I didn't act. I just let it happen.'

'So now you're to blame for his heart attack?' Logan queried harshly. 'What would you have done to prevent it? Kent Madden was never a man to listen to reason. He only ever considered his own reasons, his own greedy schemes.'

'You don't know him! You never did!' Abigail managed hotly, stung into life by the harsh, condemning tone.

'I know every last thing about him,' Logan growled. 'I know every detail of his life up to the present moment. When I turn my gaze on somebody they don't have much that remains hidden.'

CHAPTER FOUR

ABIGAIL met the cold gaze now, the icy glitter of eyes that had once smiled at her. Had she ever really known this man? Had she really been his wife in every sense of the word?

'I wonder how much you found out from me?' she murmured shakily. 'I suppose I told you plenty without even knowing it. Now he's dying—'

'And once again you're taking the blame,' Logan cut in impatiently. His mouth suddenly twisted coldly. 'Or is the balance tilting? Is it getting round to my turn? He would never have reached this stage if I hadn't been intent on crushing him. Is that where we're settling now?'

'Who knows what would have happened?' Abigail whispered, her eyes intent on her own, trembling hands. 'If any of us could see the future how differently we would act.' She looked up at him. 'But not you, Logan. You would never have acted differently, would you?' His face seemed to swim before her eyes and she blinked rapidly. 'This drink has gone straight to my head.'

'You need food,' Logan said curtly. It was served at that moment and when she just looked at it blankly he handed her her knife and fork. 'Eat,' he bit out. 'You don't move until I've seen you eat. You need sleep too but the food comes first.'

'I can't sleep,' Abigail pointed out shakily, eating as ordered even though she didn't feel at all like it. 'I'll sit on the bench at the hospital and try to rest a bit.'

'You'll get into bed and sleep. When you've finished this you're going to the flat.'

'What flat?' Abigail looked up with startled eyes and he stared back at her grimly.

'*Our* flat. We've only ever had the one and it's still there.'

'It's yours. It has nothing to do with me.' There was a faint trace of panic at the back of her voice but if he heard it Logan gave no sign. Instead he regarded her steadily, almost patiently.

'When you married me,' he reminded her quietly, 'half of everything I had became yours. That included the flat, the house and everything else. If you don't want to sleep in my half of the flat you can sleep in your half.'

'This isn't the time to be amusing,' Abigail remonstrated chokily, and he eyed her with a certain amount of disparagement.

'I'm telling you the facts, not trying to entertain you. If you had divorced me you would by now be quite wealthy. If I die first you'll be rolling in money.'

'Stop it!' Abigail said sharply. 'I want nothing of yours at all and you know that.'

'But you'll get it, Abbie,' he promised softly. 'You're probably old enough to handle wealth by now.'

'Get married again!' Abigail suggested rather desperately. She wanted this taunting conversation to stop because she knew it was just that. Logan was taunting her even though her father was lying in a stiff white bed and clinging onto life.

'I have a wife,' he pointed out coldly, the derision leaving his eyes. 'One catastrophic marriage is enough for me. I don't need any more loose ends to tie off.'

'If my father dies it will be one thing finished,' Abigail muttered bitterly, and she finished her food, and he stood with one impatient movement, drawing her sharply to her feet.

'The conversation is over, Abigail. Now you sleep!'

'I will not!' For a second she stood her ground but he could never have had any doubt about winning. She was dazed, swaying, out on her feet. Stress, tiredness and then the unexpected wine had all done their bit. She could have slept on the table with no difficulty.

'Walk to the car or I'll carry you,' he warned, and she managed to get to the door, the sight of the Jaguar like the light at the end of a tunnel. Wherever Logan was taking her she was going to go because she could not stay upright for very much longer.

'My father...' she began, and his hand came under her elbow, supporting her as she moved uncertainly forward.

'Leave that to me. I'll not let you down,' he assured her. He never had actually. She ran that thought hazily through her mind. Logan had never let her down. Except, of course, with Fenella Mitchell. The thought of that kept her awake until they were in the flat that had once been so thrillingly familiar.

How many times since she had left him had Logan brought Fenella here? If Fenella wanted a baby would he refuse her too? Of course, Fenella would not want children, but *she* had wanted Logan's child—wanted it so badly.

'Why?' she whispered. She stood swaying as Logan shut the door behind them. 'Why couldn't I have a baby?'

He turned swiftly at the pained sound of her voice, his gaze sharpening as he saw the few tears on her cheeks. They were tears of regret. If there had been a baby she would have had something, someone, some part of Logan.

'You're tired, Abigail.' His voice was curiously husky and she looked across at him mournfully.

'Why?' she repeated in the same whisper. 'I never did understand. I wanted a baby. What harm could it have done, even though you never intended to stay married to me, even though you were merely after my father?'

Logan's face tightened and he walked slowly towards her, taking her jacket and tossing it down on a chair.

'You need some sleep. This is not the moment to discuss the past. Ask me again at some other time,' he suggested grimly. 'For now, go to bed. You know the way.'

'I've nothing to sleep in...' she began, but he turned away and spoke over his shoulder.

'You left everything when you fled, including your clothes. They're all still there, right where you abandoned them. As I recall, you had plenty of nighties.'

It was too much trouble to move and when she stood there staring at him Logan came back and lifted her up, taking her into the bedroom. He tossed her a nightie as she sat on the bed in a lifeless manner and his looks were a stern warning as he said, 'You undress all by yourself, otherwise I might just change my mind about that baby.'

As he walked out and closed the door firmly she still sat there staring after him, too bemused and worn out to make any sense of him at all. Sometimes it seemed that she had merely dreamed Logan, conjured him up in her head, because this man was not the Logan she remembered. She managed to get into the nightie and was asleep the moment her head touched the pillow. She was too worn out to worry any more tonight.

* * *

Next day, Abigail awoke to find herself in the flat. It was instantly familiar and frightening and she washed and dressed as quickly as she could, only to find that she was alone in the place.

There was no sign of Logan and she dared to make herself some breakfast, gulping down a few spoonfuls of cereal and then making for the phone. She had slept all night and she dreaded hearing the report from the hospital about her father.

Logan came in before she had even reached the telephone and after one swift glance at her strained face he closed the door and turned back to her.

'Your father is holding his own.'

'How do you know? Did you ring? Why didn't you wake me?'

'To what purpose? In any case, they won't let you see him.'

'Of course they will! I'm going there now, at once!' Abigail turned on him with blazing eyes, sure that he was once again trying to manoeuvre her for some dark ends of his own.

'Do so,' he agreed indifferently. 'However, they'll not let you see him.'

'Oh? How do you know?' She snapped out the question, almost ready to fly into a rage, and he glanced at her sceptically.

'I've been there already.'

The brief statement left her unable to rage at all. Logan had been there? He had tried to see her father? It was inconceivable—unless he had gone to make more mischief.

'You went to pester a man who may well by dying?' she choked. 'You went to gloat?'

'How highly you regard me, Abigail.' Logan spun round with sheer fury glittering in his eyes. 'How well trained you are. Every word your father speaks is true and just but I'm every sort of villain. Why the hell did you marry me in the first place?'

'I loved you.' It was out before she could stop it, so simply said, and it did little to calm him down.

'Childish fantasy, no doubt,' he grunted, frowning at her darkly. The rage seemed to be going and she was glad of it. She had never really seen Logan in a rage before although she had heard him with other people. 'I went to have a word with him,' Logan continued after staring at her bleakly. 'I thought it might help. You may not have registered the fact but nobody is after Kent Madden's precious firm at the moment.'

She had noticed yesterday—noticed and been scared more than ever.

'The bank,' she began nervously. 'They didn't—'

'I called the dogs off,' Logan informed her curtly. 'After you came to see me I had a rethink. I went to the hospital today to tell your father the latest news and to make my offer. I thought it might just perk him up but unfortunately they wouldn't let me near him.'

'What offer?' It was difficult to breathe, the whole situation terrifying because she knew that Logan had not just stopped his vendetta. There was something else and it could only be something worse.

'Perhaps you had better sit down,' Logan suggested, sitting himself and indicating a chair opposite, and she obeyed because by the look on his face she knew she was going to need some support.

'What offer?' she repeated, staring at him with wide green eyes that showed every one of her tumbling emotions.

'I'm prepared to stop this whole thing,' Logan stated coolly. 'I'm prepared to make an offer for the Madden Corporation and ease it into my own firm or, if he prefers it, I'm willing to help put the Madden Corporation back on its feet.'

It was impossible! He didn't mean it. Abigail watched him intently, her mind searching for snags, traps, but his face was impassive and she finally drew in a long, shuddering breath.

'Why?' she asked. It was certainly not because she had been to see him, certainly not pity for her father, but unless he was willing to tell her his reasons she had no chance of finding out. Logan was cold and ruthless now. He probably had always been like that but she had been too young and too entranced to notice it before.

'Not generosity and not from the kindness of my heart.' He leaned back, crossing one elegantly clad leg over the other, his lips turned down in a smile of sceptical amusement. 'There is one proviso.'

There would be and it would be horrifying. Abigail stared at him without speaking, afraid to ask.

'I would be very grateful if you would stop looking at me like a scared rabbit,' he remarked, the sceptical amusement touching his eyes too. 'The proviso is not too worrying, all things being considered.'

'What things?' Abigail asked breathlessly.

'I'm prepared to admit that my relentless pursuit of the firm has at least something to do with your father's present condition,' Logan conceded. 'I never wanted to see him dead. I told you that before. However, even without my malevolent interest, the Madden Corporation is finished, unless I help openly, unless I am seen to be in some sort of charge for a while. Therefore, you need me and I'm willing to help.'

'But? Abigail whispered, voicing the unspoken implication.

'I wish to borrow my wife for a few weeks. Nothing too arduous, no marital duties, merely a front for a necessary trip I'm obliged to make.'

'What?' Abigail stood slowly, holding onto the arm of the chair, and Logan looked up at her, his dark brows raised in query, the light of real mischief now sparkling in those astonishing eyes.

'You're not stupid, Abigail,' he commented quietly. 'You heard and you understood. I'm making a trip. For a few weeks I need a wife, in name only. I already have one, so what could be more simple?'

'What are you up to?' she stormed, her breath back now and her temper rising. 'Even seeing you would probably finish my father off. Any suggestion like this would do it for sure. If you need somebody with you, take Fenella Mitchell!'

'She's not my wife,' Logan pointed out smoothly, his amused eyes still on her furious face. 'I have a big business deal—a very big deal—and it's with an American company of considerable size. It's still family owned and the man who owns it has family values. He does not like the idea of divorce, mistresses or anything less wholesome than home-baked apple pie. My wife has been invited along. He knows I'm married and he expects to meet you. I'm buying him out and then I'll have another foothold in the States.'

'Then go and buy him out!' Abigail snapped. 'Just leave the Madden Corporation to sink without trace. We've been doing that very well for months.'

'He does not need the money and other people are interested,' Logan said steadily. 'I want that firm. Given my offer, however large, and an offer from a solid family man, he'll take the latter. He's funny that way.'

'This is not amusing!' she spat out. 'There's no way I'll allow you to see my father. It's very typical of you that while he's hanging onto life by a thread you're thinking of your own schemes.'

'You imagine I owe him any favours?' Logan grated, his amusement gone. 'I made a promise five years ago and so far I've kept it. I can take somebody else and chance anyone finding out. I'm making the offer to you because I never promised to see Kent Madden dead, in spite of what he did to my father and mother.'

'He did nothing!' Abigail almost screamed. 'Whatever it was, it was business.'

'He's a liar and a cheat,' Logan snapped. He stood and towered over her. 'Go to the hospital and try to take a look at him and then ring me with your decision. The offer holds only until tonight. You can make this deal yourself without telling him at all, if that's what you want. If you don't make the deal, I'll let loose the dogs again.'

'Why did you marry me?' Abigail whispered, white to the lips after her burst of rage, and he tilted her chin with one imperious finger.

'For the same reason that you married me, Abigail. I loved you, or, if you can't swallow that, I wanted you. I think I proved that at least.'

He walked out of the flat and after a few seconds she heard the low purr of the Jaguar as it pulled away. He was leaving her here, giving her time to think, and he knew she had no sort of transport.

There was no way that she would agree to this plan. She had a job lined up already with Brian Wingate. The Madden Corporation could sink in deep, murky water.

She would never go back to Logan in any way at all. She was still hurting from the last time. In this flat, the image of him here with her, her old longing to be closer to him could surface without warning. Logan was what he had always been—danger.

She got ready quickly and called a taxi. Maybe they would not let her see her father but it was something she was going to find out for herself. She could not take Logan's word for anything.

She couldn't get past the nurse on duty at the desk.

'I'm sorry, Mrs Steele. No visitors allowed. Your father is holding his own at the moment. The signs are good but he cannot have visitors. I told your husband that when he came earlier. If he had passed that message on it would have saved you a journey.'

'He did pass it on,' Abigail said frustratedly. 'Surely the restriction doesn't apply to me, though? I'm Kent Madden's daughter—family. Even if my husband couldn't see him, I surely have the right?'

She was still arguing when the ward sister appeared and the nurse on duty turned to this more commanding figure for support.

'Your husband was told—' the sister began, but Abigail interrupted her determinedly.

'I have every right to see my father! You may be able to refuse to let his son-in-law see him but you can't refuse me. I'm the next of kin.'

It made her cringe to say 'son-in-law' and she was just glad that her father could not hear the words spoken. To Kent Madden, Logan was the son-in-law from hell. He hadn't even acknowledged that she was married when things had been normal, when she had been happy with Logan.

The sister was studying her face and what she saw there seemed to soften her rather starchy resolution.

'You can look at him through the glass,' she conceded reluctantly. 'You can't enter the room and you must not try to speak to him even if he recognises you.'

'Is he still unconscious?' Abigail whispered, and the sister turned stiffly to lead her along the corridor.

'Sometimes he's awake, even fairly lucid, although it's difficult to hear the things he says.'

They came to the intensive-care unit and Abigail held herself tightly under control as the sister motioned her to walk forward to the wide glass window that restricted further passage. It was a small room with only three beds and at the moment there was only one patient there. Abigail went close to the glass and bit down on her lip in shock.

If there had been others there she would not have known which one to look at because the man in the high white bed was nothing like her father. He seemed to have grown smaller overnight. His face was as white as his hair but even that was not the cause of the unspeakable shock she felt.

He seemed almost less than human because there were tubes running from the bed and he seemed to be attached to so much machinery that to imagine him opening his eyes and being at all normal was impossible. At that moment she felt all hope disappear.

She closed her eyes, swaying dizzily, and the sister took her arm to steady her.

'It's not some cruel fancy of ours to restrict visitors, Mrs Steele,' she pointed out in a suddenly kind voice. 'Sometimes visitors can't cope with it. It's frightening for members of the family to see this sort of thing, and so unnecessary. By tomorrow or the next day your father may very well be more normal and you could have been spared the shock of this. Your husband should have prevented you from coming.'

'He—he tried to,' Abigail muttered. 'He told me I wouldn't be able to see my father.'

But she had distrusted him as usual, she reminded herself, and Logan could not have foreseen that her father would be in this state. Would he have tried to stop her coming if he had realised? It was something that was impossible to know.

'Has—has my father asked for me?' she enquired shakily as the sister led her away.

'Not to my knowledge. He's come round on several occasions but it was difficult to know how much he understood when he was awake. He was agitated each time. He talked about "the company" but it was so mixed up that I couldn't actually tell you what he said.'

'I can guess,' Abigail assured her dully. It would be all about the Madden Corporation, not about her. His life was the company and even when he hung between life and death it was the Madden Corporation that filled his mind.

Things had never been any different so why should she expect a change now? Even her mother had taken second place to the Madden Corporation. Her own place was and always had been very low on the list of priorities. If he fought to live it would not be so that he could see her again. It would be to watch his company sink into the dust.

Abigail went back to the flat and it was not until she arrived that she realised she no longer had keys to it. All those sorts of things she had thrown out when she had left Logan four years earlier and for a second she stood on the step at the front door, wondering almost in a daze what exactly she should do.

Logan opened the door as she was turning away and without a word she went in and walked past him.

'I take it that you've been to the hospital?' He came into the sitting room and stood by the door, a frown on his face as he saw her expression.

'Yes. I saw him. They—they wouldn't let me at first but I insisted. They let me go to the window and I could see . . . I could see . . .'

'You little fool!' Logan strode forward and firmly put her into a chair. Before she knew it there was a glass of brandy in her hand and Logan was standing over her as she sipped the drink. It was very obvious that she was in no condition to argue with him and after a second he went to stand by the window, staring out into the street.

'What have you gained by this visit, Abigail?' he finally asked wearily.

'I saw him.'

At the dull sound of her voice he spun round, his grey eyes blazing.

'Damn it all, Abigail!' he rasped. 'Why didn't you listen to me? Why didn't you let me take care of you? You're no more capable of stepping firmly on this earth than you ever were. God knows how you get through a day at that office. I'm not even sure how you manage to survive from minute to minute.'

'I'm not the incompetent fool you seem to imagine,' Abigail retaliated. The brandy had allowed some warmth to seep into her and she looked up at Logan with green-eyed bitterness. 'Thanks to you, I haven't a lot of choice about going in to the office. It's managing without me at this moment but that state of affairs won't last long. There's nobody there to take charge—to face things.'

'There's nothing to face right now,' Logan reminded her angrily. 'I told you I'd called off the pack. Nothing will be happening.'

'Precisely!' Abigail snapped back. 'There's no business either. Nothing happening with the bank because you stepped in. Nothing happening in the way of business because you've undermined everything. Nothing and nothing make a big fat zero!'

'Martha Bates can supervise zero adequately,' Logan growled sarcastically. 'She's not in the building alone. The staff are still working.'

'For the time being! Before long they'll all be sacked.'

'Not if I take the firm under my wing.'

Logan's voice had gone quiet and Abigail hastily looked away, scared about the decision she had been reaching ever since she had had her horrifying glimpse of her father. She had been turning things over and over in her mind and she had come to the conclusion that she had no choice at all.

Deep inside, she knew that the only way to make her father fight his way back to health was to give him something to fight for, and he would certainly not fight for her, any more than he would have done for her mother's sake. Only the firm meant anything to him. There was the Madden Corporation or there was nothing. Without Logan's power there would be no Madden Corporation.

Logan came and threw himself into the chair opposite, his startling grey eyes on her downcast face.

'What are his chances?' he asked with that astonishing way he had always had of collecting her wandering thoughts.

'Not good.' She looked up at him, her eyes almost glazed with unhappiness. 'He came round earlier. The sister told me. He—he never asked for me. He was talking about the firm.'

Logan's eyes narrowed, his glance racing across her face. His lips tightened angrily at her tragic look but his voice was perfectly even.

'He would be only semi-conscious. I imagine it's a dream-like state. Don't expect miracles, Abigail.'

'I don't think I've ever expected miracles,' she said with quiet simplicity. 'I'm too ordinary for miracles. Things like that belong to you, Logan. You drive miracles out into the open and pounce on them.'

Brief amusement flickered in his eyes at her words but he didn't smile.

'He's hanging on at any rate,' he reminded her. 'At some point he'll fight to survive. It's part of his nature.'

'It always has been,' she agreed sombrely. 'He's always had something to fight for. Now he has nothing to fight for and he certainly won't fight for me.'

Rage flared on Logan's face, his eyes flashing icy sparks, and for a second her green gaze wandered over him, searching his changing expressions. It was a question of courage after all. Did she have the courage to step back into Logan's world for a time?

For a long and wonderful year he had been everything in her life and when it had ended she had thought she would never be able to recover. In a way she never had recovered because, as she looked at him now, memory came unbidden—secretive and painful. He was still the most magnificent person she had ever seen, still the most powerful. The dark voice was now often hidden in anger but always at the back of her mind she could hear his laughter and his gentleness like some ghost from the past.

'I agree,' she said quickly before she could change her mind.

'To what?' He sat very still, watching her intently, and her face began to flush with a mixture of fright and embarrassment. For all she knew, it had been some cruel joke. For all she knew, he might very well have changed his mind.

'You—you wanted to—to borrow me,' she managed to stammer. 'You wanted to make a bargain with my father.'

'So I did,' Logan agreed, his voice a dark murmur. 'I never got to see him, though, and even if I had it's clear that he would not have been in any condition to barter.'

'Why are you like this?' Abigail flared, and he looked at her coolly.

'Maybe I was born like this. Or maybe I grew into it, propelled by the force of circumstance. Whatever the reason, I'm now set in my ways, as they say.' He sat back and crossed one ankle over his knee, his head thrown back as he watched her through half-closed eyes. 'I take it that you're prepared to make the bargain yourself. A unilateral decision?'

'I have no choice.' She avoided his gaze, her own eyes on the slender length of her fingers. She dared not look up and see his answer on his face. 'I have to give my father some reason to live.'

He was silent for a long time and still she didn't look up. She was just beginning to think that he would never answer when he suddenly stood and looked down at her.

'Very well. I accept the arrangement. You pretend to be my wife again—'

'I was never pretending!' Abigail almost shouted, her head snapping up as she stared at him angrily. 'The pretence was all yours! I never tried to damage anyone you cared about and *I* never had a secret lover!'

'I believe you,' Logan murmured sardonically. 'As I understand it, you've moved into that sphere since you left me. Brian Wingate, isn't it?'

'Yes!' Abigail lied vehemently. Let him think what he liked. If he imagined she had somebody else he would, perhaps, stand clear of her until this charade was over. 'Let me remind you, though, that Brian and I didn't even know each other when I was married to you.'

'You're still married to me, sweetheart,' Logan said with quiet acidity. 'Tell him to keep that in mind. Tell him to keep his distance, too. As far as everyone is concerned, we're reconciled until this is all over. If one word of this being a sham reaches my American contacts, the whole deal will be off, and if *my* deal is off, Abigail, then so is yours.'

She stood and began to collect her things. There was nothing she could do at the moment about seeing her father and she had no intention of staying here.

'Where are you going?' Logan snapped, his hand coming like a vice round her wrist.

'Home. Where else?' she asked coldly. 'No doubt you'll give me the date when this thing is to begin. I assure you that I'll be on the starting line, ready and waiting.'

'Going back to the house is not a good idea,' Logan stated more quietly, and she looked at him scornfully. 'You need someone with you.'

'Oh, no, you don't Logan. I'm not nineteen now. There's no way you're getting me under your thumb again. We've got a bargain and I want some concrete proof before this bargain begins.'

'It's already begun,' he said softly, his hand falling away from her wrist. 'It had begun before I even mentioned any sort of deal. I called off the bank. As to my

keeping my end of the bargain, you have my word,
Abigail.'

It stopped her angry attack and knocked the force out
of her argument. Logan's word was and always had been
good enough for anyone.

'Very well,' she agreed, 'but at the moment there's no
need for me to be here.'

'We're close to the hospital,' he reminded her. 'If your
father wakes up and asks for you then you'll be able to
be there in minutes. If anything happens to him, you'll
also be on call,' he added quietly.

Abigail knew it was true. She also knew that her own
thoughts about her father's chances of survival were
running on those lines. Hearing Logan put them into
words was too much, though, and she flew at him, tears
streaming down her cheeks.

'You pig!' she shouted, her hands flying to his face,
her eyes overflowing. 'That's what you want, isn't it?
You're watching like some ferocious hunting animal,
waiting for him to die!'

Logan caught her as she attacked him, his strong hands
easily subduing her, pinning her arms to her sides, his
grip on her long, black hair forcing her head up.

'I am not waiting for him to die!' he grated furiously.
'It's a matter of common sense and, my Lord, you've
little of that. When he collapsed you had nobody,
Abigail, and let me remind you that you still have
nobody. You have me, and without me you're alone.'

The words sank in like acid, taking away her anger
and her much needed self-possession. When had she ever
had anyone but Logan? And she had never even really
had him. The angry tension left her body and she slowly
sagged, her shoulders drooping under his biting grip,
tears still glistening on her lashes.

'All right,' she whispered. 'I'll stay but I—I can't stay here if you're here.'

'I never thought you would. I'll move out, providing that we have an understanding—if anything happens, you ring me and let me know. I want to look after you. Whatever you feel about me, you need me.'

Abigail nodded, her head down now to hide her tear-stained face.

'I'll ring,' she promised. 'Where will you...?'

'I'll be at the house,' he informed her tightly. 'Our house. Remember, Abbie?'

'I've got the number somewhere,' she murmured, deliberately misunderstanding him. 'If anything happens... And—and I'll be ready when you want me.'

He suddenly caught her to him, his arms wrapping round her like iron, crushing her close with little thought to her comfort.

'When I want you?' he said vehemently. 'Abbie! I've always wanted you. Some things stay constant no matter what happens in this world, and that's one of them.'

His grip was punishing and when she dared to meet his eyes their clear grey was blazing with anger. She tried to escape but he merely tightened his grip until she gasped. There was fright on her face and he let her go, turning away in self-disgust.

'Fear not, Abigail,' he muttered with sudden cold detachment. 'You had me racing round after you like an idiot teenager once upon a time. I'm not about to repeat my mistake. This is a deal—a business deal—and when it's over you can have that divorce you've so fastidiously avoided.'

CHAPTER FIVE

LOGAN walked out of the door, slamming it behind him, and Abigail remained exactly where he had left her. She was too shaken to think straight. He was going to the house—the house she had once helped to set up in a dreamy state of happiness.

How long ago it seemed now. She sank to the chair, shaking and anxious. It would not be easy to pretend to be a happy wife to Logan. Mostly she would have to rely on his own acting ability. She would have to look at her clothes, think things out a little better. Where Logan went there was wealth and although she had lived with wealth for most of her life it had never been on a level with Logan's.

There was this trip to America. There would be glamorous people—the sort of people he was used to. Without warning she was back to long-ago, to almost five years ago, and she closed her eyes in anguish when she realised that she was once again skirting on the edge of jealousy, her self-confidence shattering at the thought of Logan with some sophisticated woman she had never even seen.

Why did he insist on taking care of her when it had all been over for four weary years? Perhaps it was masculine pride. She was still his wife and if they had separated and still been friends it would have been natural to turn to him. It was natural now but she dared not admit it. She had carried every burden alone for so long that to lean on Logan and accept his strength would wipe away all her fight.

* * *

Kent Madden began to recover during the next few days. The hospital rang to tell Abigail that he was conscious and asking for her and she went along to see him without contacting Logan at all.

Her father was weak and still frighteningly vulnerable but he was awake and looked as if he would start to fight his way out of this.

'What's happening?'

Abigail hid a weary smile. It was exactly what she had expected and she made no attempt to misunderstand him. He did not mean what was happening in her own life. He was not aware of the momentous changes she was planning to face. He merely wanted to know about the firm, and she settled down to tell him although there was nothing concrete to relate.

'Nothing much. Everything seems to be quiet. The bank has backed off, if that's what you mean.'

'Why?' He was instantly suspicious, agitated and she tried to skirt around the necessity to tell him. In fact she was in a dilemma. If she simply shrugged and said she didn't know then he would go on worrying. If she told him that Logan had softened he just wouldn't believe it.

She dared not take the risk of telling him about her agreement with Logan either because there was so much hatred between them that any surge of such an emotion could put her father right back to where he had been.

'Well, business is still coming in,' she answered vaguely. 'Perhaps they're having second thoughts.'

'Abigail, you're hopeless,' he snapped. 'Banks don't have second thoughts. It's all profit and loss to them and they saw a good while ago that we come on the loss side.' He was silent, thinking it over. 'There's something peculiar going on,' he finally concluded.

Abigail could see that he was getting upset and she looked at him carefully, trying to make up her mind. Luckily she didn't have to come to any decision because the sister appeared and ushered her out. The brief visit was over and Sister wanted to talk to her.

'He needs surgery,' she began when they were in her office. 'The surgeon has spoken to your father and explained things to him. He needs a triple bypass operation. That's his only way back to any sort of normal health. After that he needs rest and careful nursing for a while and then, with any luck, you should be able to have him back at home with you.'

'Does he agree to all this?' Abigail asked, her heart lurching at the thought of such a big operation. Her father had not mentioned one word about it to her. All he had been concerned with was business.

'Yes, he does. He doesn't even seem to be unduly anxious either.' The sister suddenly smiled. 'I really think he just wants to get back to work.'

Abigail nodded. She knew that. She also knew that he would take no precautions and would live the same life he had always lived—too much worry, too much drink and too much food. However, he had agreed all by himself—'unilaterally', as Logan had said to her. It was out of her hands and all she had to do was wait for the day to arrive.

It arrived two weeks later. Until that time she didn't see Logan. She had promised to get in touch with him if anything happened but she did not. Seeing him was too risky a proposition and she wanted to keep him out of her life until the very last moment, until she actually had to keep her end of the bargain.

She saw her father each day but talking to him was quite a strain. Abigail was always aware that at any moment he might say something that would force her into a confession about her agreement with Logan.

The night before the operation he seemed to be much stronger. Once again he was questioning her, wanting to know what was going on, and this time she decided to take the risk and tell him. The thought of going back to his office was making him more vigorous and she had to let him know that there was more hope than just the vague thought of the bank being in a kindly frame of mind.

'Logan called off the bank,' she said quietly, watching him for any adverse reaction. 'He tried to see you to tell you but you were too ill.'

At the mention of Logan's name her father's face was suffused with colour and she clasped his hand anxiously.

'It's all right,' she assured him quickly. 'He didn't want to see anything happen to you.'

'You believe that?' Her father gave an angry bark of laughter. 'He always bamboozled you, girl. He had you wound round his finger and you're falling for the same old tricks. If the bank stepped back it's nothing to do with Steele.'

Abigail was suddenly angry. She was angry at the constant battering of her self-esteem by both Logan and her father, angry at the way she had to take the blows and still get none of the praise.

'Logan called them off,' she said steadily. 'It's not only the bank. He's called off all the creditors. Things are in limbo but at least nothing is getting worse. He called them off because—because he has a bargain with me.'

'What bargain?' Kent Madden leaned forward in his bed and glared at her. 'What sort of bargain would a man like that make? And even if he did he'd never honour it.'

The word 'honour' seemed to sit uneasily on his tongue and Abigail looked at him sharply. In spite of everything she trusted Logan and she knew without any doubt at all that he would hold to his word whatever happened.

'I'm going to America with him when you're better,' she told her father firmly. 'I'm going as—as his hostess.' At the last moment she shied off from saying his wife. That would have been too much for her father to take. 'He has a deal there and he needs me. In return he's offered to take the Madden Corporation under his wing, either to buy us out or to get it on its feet to hand it back to us. He'll agree to whatever you decide and he'll also make it known that he's involved. That would make us reasonably viable again and take all the heat off.'

Abigail finished in a breathless rush, anxiously watching her father's face, and he lay back against the pillows, his high colour fading, his eyes narrowed and calculating.

'He wants you back?' he finally asked, and Abigail shook her head decidedly.

'Definitely not! I wouldn't go in any case but that's not what he wants at all. It's just a cover for a business deal and when it's over he suggests that I get a divorce.'

Kent Madden's head shot up at that and he looked at her closely again.

'It must be a big deal,' he probed quietly.

'It is. It's another foothold in America and he doesn't want it to fall through. Apparently the man involved doesn't like anyone of Logan's age to be unattached. He's old-fashioned.'

'So you're going as his wife.' Her father said that flatly, still watching her, no sign of anger or outrage on his face.

'In name only,' she assured him quickly, and he nodded thoughtfully.

'We've nothing to lose and everything to gain,' he pronounced after a second's thought. He smiled for the first time, a light in his eyes that she didn't exactly like. 'Go ahead, Abigail. It will get the firm right off the hook. Good girl.'

It made her feel even worse, even more valueless, and as she left he made one more comment that put the whole thing into a new light.

'You're still his wife, after all.'

Yes. It was all right to be Logan's wife if it was useful to the Madden Corporation. If there had not been this bitterness between Logan and her father, Kent Madden would have welcomed his new son-in-law with open arms five years ago. He would have seen it as a decided advantage to the firm. That was what it all boiled down to, and she left feeling like a mere commodity to be moved at will by two powerful men who looked over her head and disregarded her as a person.

Logan phoned that night to ask about her father and she had to tell him about the operation. He was silent for a minute.

'It seems to me that we had agreed that if anything happened you would contact me,' he said icily.

'Nothing happened. I didn't think you wanted bothering with every detail.'

'What you mean is that you wanted to make damned sure that I had no excuse for being anywhere near you,' he grated. 'When is this operation taking place?' he finished angrily.

'Tomorrow.' Before he could say that he would go to the hospital with her she told him about her conversation with her father. 'I told him about—about our bargain,' she said quickly.

'And?' Logan seemed to be very still and quiet; even over the telephone she could detect that.

'He seems to think it's a good idea.'

She heard Logan laugh—a cold, harsh sound that had her hand tightening on the receiver. 'I can well believe it,' he assured her acidly. 'He does realise, I hope, that it will necessitate you being out of the country?'

'I told him all that but—but I can't go before he has his operation.'

'Do you think I would expect you to, Abigail?' he murmured softly. 'I want a happy, smiling wife with me, not some wistful creature who's looking over her shoulder all the time, expecting bad news. We can wait until this is over. We'll go as soon as we know he's safe.'

'Thank you.' She said it quietly and this time when he laughed the anger had gone. She could imagine his grey eyes sparkling and the thought of them brought a slow flush to her cheeks.

'You're welcome, Mrs Steele,' he told her mockingly. She just kept quiet and his voice dropped into the familiar dark sound. 'I give up on you, Abbie. You'll obviously never toughen up. In all probability I'll spend most of my trip to America watching to see that nobody upsets you.'

'I can take care of myself!' she managed sharply, and his laughter was even more amused.

'Well, we can pretend. Providing that I'm right beside you, we can pretend anything.'

Abigail simply rang off, glad to cut off the sound of his voice. The old familiar shivers were running over her skin and she walked about the flat for ages, berating herself.

'I will not fall for anything again!' she told herself fiercely. 'I will not let Logan get to me.'

It was a panicky reaction to his voice, just as she had felt a panicky reaction to his presence before. And who was she fooling anyway? The reason she had not contacted him and asked him to go with her to the hospital was not that she had not needed his support, it was because she had felt too vulnerable to have him around.

Even the way he had grabbed her and held her roughly the last time she had seen him had lingered in her mind. He was always there, right at the back of her thoughts, and the sooner she was able to be entirely free of him, the safer she would be.

The operation went smoothly with no trouble at all. Apparently, apart from his heart condition, her father was still a tough and strong man. The surgeon told her that later. At the last minute she had telephoned Logan and told him the time of the operation, and when she'd arrived Logan had already been there. He waited with her throughout the long operation and although he said very little it gave her courage to look up and see him reading a paper or wandering around watching the hospital in progress. He was like a rock, immovable, strong, and she had never doubted that.

Afterwards he took her out for a meal and that night Abigail slept more peacefully than she had slept for a long time. Logan's quiet presence had soothed her like a drug. For just one short time there had been safety.

It was only the next day that she was sufficiently back in the world to realise that this was it. Now there was nothing to stop Logan making his arrangements for the trip to America. She had leaned on his strength, accepted his help both with the firm and with her own problems. Now she had to pay the price and keep her side of the bargain.

Going in to work could not be put off any longer and although there was still an uneasy atmosphere in the building it was possible to sense, with no words spoken, that everyone knew things had changed.

'Logan is helping,' she told Martha. In all fairness she had to tell Martha something and the truth had always seemed best to Abigail.

'About time too,' Martha sniffed, but it didn't take any crystal ball to see that she was delighted. She asked no questions and Abigail offered no further comments. If Martha wanted to believe that they were back together again she would find out sooner or later that it was all a business deal.

'I have to go to America,' she offered a little distantly, and to her surprise Martha took that well too, with no questions.

'Things will still be here when you get back,' she said comfortably, and Abigail pretended not to see the pleased gleam in her eyes. It seemed that she was not the only one who could relapse into dreams. Martha suffered from the same disease as far as Logan was concerned.

'By the way,' she added as Abigail was about to go to her office, 'Brian Wingate phoned. He's back from Germany sooner than he expected.'

'Fine.' Abigail smiled slightly and walked off. Another problem. She hid her sudden frown. There was the little matter of his offer of a job and there was the somewhat bigger matter of her lie about him to Logan.

Still, it was not important. The two would never meet, and she would contact Brian as soon as this deal with Logan was over because quite clearly she would need that job. She had no intention of working here with Logan constantly in and out as he set the firm to rights. She also had no intention of being tossed this way and that by every whim of her father. If he wanted to come back here and work with Logan he was welcome to try it.

For the first time in a long time, Abigail enjoyed the day at work. For some reason a weight seemed to have lifted from her and she did not know whether it was the promise of Logan taking over or if her new determination to stand alone had something to do with it.

She left the office with a smile on her face. Now that her father was off the danger list there was no need at all to stay at the flat and she had her own car with her. Tonight she intended to go home, make arrangements with Rose and acquaint her with all the facts.

She was just approaching her car when Brian drew up and sounded his horn, stopping her in her tracks. He wound the window down and shouted before he had even got out of his car.

'Abigail, love! I'm back! You can stop worrying. Rescue is here.'

She turned at the sound of his voice, laughing towards him, glad to see his warm-looking face peering at her from the open window of the car, his fair hair untidy as if he had been in a strong breeze. Her laughter faded, however, when the familiar dark Jaguar pulled in silently behind Brian's more modest vehicle and Logan sat watching events with icy eyes and a mouth tightened in anger.

Before she could take any action, an unsuspecting Brian had leapt from his car and hurried over to give her a great hug and to kiss her soundly—a thing he had never done before in the whole time she had known him.

'I came tearing back from Germany as soon as I could,' he told her eagerly. 'I've been worrying about you all the time. Now we can plan your future.'

Abigail stood like someone stunned. Dimly she heard the dull thud of the Jaguar door closing and she knew that somewhere very close Logan was on his feet and moving towards them. For herself, she was powerless to move. All her calm thoughts in the safety of the office had now vanished. Logan was about to meet Brian face to face and he would readily believe her lie now after Brian's unrestrained show of affection.

Embarrassment held her to the spot and it was only as she stared over Brian's shoulder, watching Logan's approach with wide and anxious eyes, that Brian sensed some strain in the atmosphere.

'What is it, love?' he asked in a puzzled voice. Brian had a boisterous voice that carried and she wondered desperately how much Logan had heard of his greeting. 'There's no need to worry now. You'll come to me and everything will be all right. The firm can go hang.'

He meant, of course, that she would be working for him but she could tell by the thunder on Logan's face that he had misunderstood.

'Abigail is overwhelmed,' Logan assured him as he came up to them. His voice was as icy as his eyes and Brian spun round almost open-mouthed. 'However,' Logan continued, 'the firm will not go hang and my wife will not come to you. She has a future that does not even contain a glimpse of you.'

'You're back together?' Brian stared at him, too stunned to be afraid of the anger in those cold eyes.

'Oh, yes,' Logan assured him sarcastically. 'I'm sure if you had given her half a chance she would have told you. Next week we're going to America—a second honeymoon.' He paused and looked from his greater height into Brian's astonished face. 'Don't make the mistake of trying to see her again.'

He took Abigail's arm in a tight grip and before she could react she was being moved forcibly towards the Jaguar.

'Let me go!' Even now, embarrassment kept her voice low, and Logan stopped, looking down at her with wild anger on his face.

'If I let you go, my dear Abigail, I also let the firm go. It will drop from a great height and be smashed. The bank will catch the worthwhile pieces and by the time your father leaves hospital there will not even be the dust to sweep up.'

'You promised!' Abigail stared up at him, her expression a mixture of anger and fear. She'd had one day of relief from strain and now she was being propelled back into it.

'And I keep my promises, as you know,' Logan reminded her harshly. 'We have a deal. All by yourself you struck a bargain with me and I made it clear that should anyone even begin to imagine that it was a sham then the deal would be off. Moving in with Wingate would be a fairly strong way of proving that we are not at all reconciled. From that moment on, you would be no use to me at all. I would not feel obliged to keep my end of the bargain.'

'You—you got it all wrong,' Abigail began urgently. 'You misunderstood.'

'Did I?' Logan asked violently. 'You've already admitted that Wingate is your lover and now he holds you tight and announces that you'll go with him, everything will be all right. Maybe we don't need each other after all; maybe this bargain should be called off right now.'

'He didn't mean that! He meant to go and work for him. He offered me a job before he went away.' She was about to say that Brian had never even kissed her before but she thought better of it. Pointing out a previous lie would hardly make Logan believe her now.

Logan looked down at her icily, his crystal eyes searching her face. Fury was racing just below his expression and she could see it clearly. She clenched her hands together, anxiety written all over her, and Logan watched her intently. His eyes went from her face to her tightly clenched fingers and then he took a deep, angry breath.

'Very well. We go on from here, but one false move, Abigail, and I call off the deal. Any sign of Wingate and you're on your own; so is the Madden Corporation.'

He began to lead her away again, straight to his car, but Abigail pulled free and faced him.

'I have my own car. I'm going back home tonight. When you want this thing to start you'll let me know. In the meantime, I have things to do. Rose is alone at the house and I can't go rushing off without making arrangements.'

'And what about Wingate?' Logan snapped caustically. 'Does he go with you when you drive off?'

'He does not!' she stormed, her patience at an end. 'I don't need a third man under my feet. Between you and my father I have plenty of trouble and none of it anything to do with me. You said that all this did not include me. Can you say that honestly now, Logan? I'm sick of being pig-in-the-middle. When this is over, you and my father can go into a room and throw mud at each other for all I care. In the meantime, I'll keep the bargain, but only on civilised terms. If you don't understand the word "civilised" then let the Madden Corporation drop from this great height you're threatening and I'll be free at last!'

Logan watched her silently for a second, his eyes lit by a sort of amused admiration.

'So, you finally grew up, Abigail,' he said softly. 'You're prepared to take on the two wolves in your life and vanquish them.'

'I just want to see the back of them both!' Abigail flared. 'Even the most humble worm can turn.'

'You were never humble,' Logan mused, 'just too sweet for your own good.' His hand reached out and touched her face lightly, his eyes skimming over her. 'Sweet, sweet Abigail,' he murmured. 'I'll take a lot of convincing that the sweetness has gone.'

'It should be quite easy to prove,' she assured him tartly. The way he touched her, the words he used combined to bring back the past and she could have done without that. 'Let me know when I'm on duty,' she finished, turning away to go to her car.

'If there's anything you need...' Logan began, and she turned flashing green eyes on him.

'Space!' she snapped. 'That's all I need from you.'

'You'll get it,' Logan promised, the amused indulgence dying from his voice. 'When this is over you'll want that divorce. After that there'll be all the space you require.'

She marched off, afraid to ask herself why his words had sent cold fingers racing over her heart. It would be the end of Logan altogether and she was too honest to hide from the realisation that there hadn't yet been an end. He had always been there, right at the back of her mind. After this he would have to be obliterated. They would both be free.

A vision of Fenella Mitchell came into her head and she suddenly knew why after all this time he was mentioning divorce. He couldn't tell her outright because she might have refused to go to the States with him. He couldn't marry Fenella quickly and take her there because it would probably upset his deal if the man knew he was divorced and remarried.

Pain seemed to race across her, tightening her chest, and she almost walked past Brian without seeing him. He was still there, beside his car, and he stopped her, his touch on her arm making her spin round and notice him.

'Is it true, Abigail? Are you two together again?'

Oh, lies, lies, lies, Abigail mourned silently. She longed to tell him the truth but if she did there would be nothing left for her father when he came out of hospital, not even the dust to sweep up, as Logan had threatened.

'We're going to try,' she managed, her face pale and distant. 'I'm sorry about all that, Brian. Logan completely misunderstood the situation.'

'I hope I haven't messed things up,' he said ruefully. 'I could see you having a go at each other.'

'It's all right,' she soothed, forcing a smile. 'Logan can get very angry for very little and, as I say, he mistook the situation.'

'I can understand him being jealous,' Brian said wryly. 'I rather put my foot in it and you know I was only being my usual blundering self.'

'You were simply being kind,' Abigail assured him. 'I'll have to go now. Rose is expecting me home. I have a lot to do before we leave for America.'

She summoned up a brilliant smile and turned away to her car. Logan jealous? He was simply enraged that his well-laid plans were in danger of being thwarted. When this was over he would hand her over to almost anyone without a qualm and go off to Fenella Mitchell.

She started the car and swung into a turn to leave the parking area and her lips tightened as she saw Logan still standing by the Jaguar, his eyes watchful. He wasn't taking any chances. If Brian turned his car to follow, Logan would probably ram him off the road.

Her father had been right. This deal in America must be very important. Logan was prepared to do almost anything to see that it did not collapse. He was taking the Madden Corporation under his wing and he was putting his private life on hold to take a respectable wife with him. Until she stepped clear of both Logan and her father she would never be anything at all but the pawn she had always been.

Logan waited until her father was safely out of hospital and tucked away in a private hospital for convalescence. It was closer to home and Rose would be able to see to taking things in that he needed. His friends would be able to visit him too, and when Abigail went he was looking better than she had seen him look for months.

'I have to go with Logan,' she reminded him. 'I don't like leaving you alone but unless I go the deal will be off. He's no more flexible about things than he has ever been.'

'He must be flexible to a certain extent, otherwise he wouldn't have been prepared to wait until I was out of hospital,' Kent Madden pointed out. 'He must have a soft spot for you. Just remember that he's a very wealthy man. Try to play your cards better this time round.'

Abigail nearly pulled out of the whole thing right then. She was only doing this for her father and she knew the danger that awaited her. Logan still had an almost mystical hold on her and the only way she could protect herself was by fighting it. Now her father was suggesting that she cast aside all her standards and patch things up with Logan in order to get some of his money.

She had difficulty in not showing her disgust openly.

'Waiting was part of the bargain,' she informed him tightly. 'He knew I wouldn't go unless I knew you were safe and getting better.'

'I've never needed anyone to prop *me* up,' her father snapped. 'Getting help for the firm is more important than hanging around here and bringing me flowers. Just put me out of your mind, Abigail, and remember all the time why you're doing this.'

'I could hardly forget,' she reminded him drily. 'I'm going to America to live a lie for as long as Logan specifies.'

'Hardly a lie,' her father corrected her with a knowing smile. 'You're going to act as his wife. You *are* his wife. He's got a lot of sense after all.'

A lot of cunning, Abigail thought bitterly as she left the hospital. Logan's cunning was almost matched by her father's callous schemes. She counted for nothing at all, being merely a useful daughter and a virtuous wife. Just once she would like to do something wild and unexpected, something for herself alone. But she was well and truly trapped. Not after this, she thought angrily. After this she would change completely. She would work for Brian, alter all her ways, be more like the Fenella Mitchells of this world.

She smiled ruefully. Who was she trying to fool? Nothing would change her. Her only hope was escape and that was what she would have the moment they came back from America. She would leave her father to his precious firm and leave Logan to live his life as he had always lived it. She had been right when she had first seen him five years ago. He was way, way beyond her, outside her world. It had merely been a dream.

CHAPTER SIX

LOGAN rang a few days later while she was in the office. The time had come and her heart thumped alarmingly when he said that they were leaving at the end of the week.

'It gives you three days to complete your preparations,' he told her inflexibly. 'We fly out on Saturday afternoon and have a stop-over in New York before flying to California.'

She had visions of beautiful, sun-bronzed women in skimpy bikinis and any bit of self-assurance she had gained by long and determined arguments with herself fled at the thought.

'Why there?' she asked shakily, and Logan sounded surprised.

'He lives there.'

'You mean we're staying at his house—his home?' Abigail gasped.

She heard Logan's low growl of exasperation before he said, 'We are not. The hospitality was offered but I refused.'

'Why?' Quivering suspicion raced over her and it was evident in her voice. Logan lost patience and snapped at her immediately.

'Not for any devious motives concerning you! This is a business trip, not a furtive, sensual weekend away.'

'Are we just going for the weekend?' Abigail muttered, her face crimson at his reprimand, and he almost exploded with frustration at her stupidity.

'We're going for as long as it takes to make the deal. Get a grip on yourself, Abigail! I have no intention of demanding my rights as a husband. My interest is purely business and it will take all your intelligence to play the part of a normal wife without any other problems. I'll collect you at your house on Saturday morning.'

'It's not necessary. I'll come by myself. If you'll just tell me the time of—'

Logan slammed down the phone before she could finish and Abigail stared at it a little desperately. He would come for her. Thank goodness her father would not be there. They had not met since the wedding five years ago and in spite of the change in Logan's attitude she would not like to think what would happen if they ever met again.

The word 'California' came floating back into her head and she stood by her desk, her mind frantically considering her wardrobe and its contents. Would she be smart enough? There would be dinner parties, perhaps. She would be meeting these people socially or it would not have been necessary for Logan to take her with him.

He had said that the man liked things to be homely. What did that mean? His having morals as homely as apple pie did not mean that his wife or the other women there would be wearing gingham dresses and hair-bands. Her only knowledge of California came from films and although she knew she was being fairly idiotic the pictures that flashed into her mind unnerved her.

Abigail abandoned the office early and told Martha that she would not be in again until she had come back from America.

'Good luck!' Martha said cheerfully. 'Have a wonderful time.' Abigail looked at her as if she were mad. It would be the most stressful time of her life. She had to play a part and that would not be easy. She was herself and had never tried to be different. She would be in daily close contact with Logan and although she trusted his word completely she did not entirely trust her own emotions. His hold on her had always been strong and she was not foolish enough to imagine that she could resist any charm.

She shrugged angrily. What charm? Logan still felt that he had the right to dictate to her, still felt he had the right to lose his temper. If she had possessed even one scrap of common sense she would have fallen in love with Brian and lived an easygoing, amusing life. Brian was like that. He did not have the raw power and unfailing physical perfection of Logan. Any contact with Logan was like a contact with live electricity.

Over the next two days she fussed endlessly over her possessions. Her father had never stinted on her allowance even when she'd been younger, and since she had been working she had amassed a lot of expensive clothes. She thought with a pang of regret about her clothes at the flat. There were beautiful things there and she had just walked out and left them.

When she had been with Logan they had travelled overseas and been out regularly to all the smart places in London. Logan had simply piled things on her, spoiling her all the time, enjoying seeing her face when he came home with something new and glamorous for her.

Glamour was what she needed now and Abigail sat down on the edge of her bed and wondered if she had the nerve to go and raid the flat. She had a key. After that first fiasco when she had almost not been able to get in, she had put a spare key in her bag. Logan was staying at the house. He wouldn't even know she had been back to the flat until he saw the clothes she was wearing. He probably wouldn't even remember them. His memories would be of Fenella's clothes.

It was that last thought that launched her into action. Why not? The clothes were still hers and so was the jewellery. She left the house in the late afternoon and drove to London to get them.

There was an unnatural darkness about the afternoon when she pulled up outside the flat and Abigail glanced at the sky to see black clouds gathering. She frowned at them and then ran up the steps to the door. She didn't want to be caught in a downpour. This would have to be a quick raid but she already knew what she would take away with her.

The silence was a little alarming as she stepped into the quiet of the flat, because it was a silence laced with memories and every one of them about Logan. She shrugged them off, took off her coat and went determinedly to the bedroom. When she had been here last she had been too filled with anxiety about her father to let any atmosphere really sink into her mind but now it was different.

The whole place sang of Logan and she knew without being told that since she had left him four years ago he had spent most of his time here. Maybe he had stayed here because the house irritated him. After all, this place had been his before he had met her but the house they had chosen together and made into a home together. This had really always been Logan's place and it still was.

She squashed maudlin thoughts about any women he might have brought here since she had left. This was not the time to allow herself to sink into any kind of emotional crisis. And there would have been just one woman in any case. She already knew who that was.

Abigail marched resolutely to the bedroom, her eyes turned only on the door to the dressing room that had been hers. There was a huge walk-in wardrobe in there and it was filled with necessities. She had neither the time, the money nor the inclination to go on some exhausting shopping spree. Everything she needed would be right here and all she had to do was collect the things and take them home to pack.

At first it was easy. The clothes, dresses, suits and gowns were still in the same pristine condition and she began to select things briskly, putting them on the end of the bed. She had no idea how long they would be staying so the selection she took had to be carefully thought out. Her initial panic-stricken notion—to scoop up the lot and depart—had to be curbed.

After much thought and consideration, though, she calmed down, and from time to time it was necessary to try on a few things. Her slender figure had not altered one bit in the past four years but perhaps now some things would not suit her more subdued appearance.

Far from not suiting, they threw her back into the glow she had once felt. The colours lit up her face and after a while a smile warmed her lips as she regained the confidence that she had grown into with Logan. She began a methodical trying-on of everything she had selected and the clothes she had arrived in were left tossed over the back of a chair.

Abigail had only a vague realisation that the threatened rain had started. Then one quick glance at the bedroom window assured her that it was already pounding down. She tossed a bright red raincoat onto the growing pile of clothes. It might not rain in California but she was taking no chances. She gave a little giggle at the thought and that was when a noise behind her alerted her to the fact that she was no longer alone in the silent flat.

She spun round, her green eyes wide with alarm, and saw that Logan was leaning indolently against the open bedroom door, his eyes moving over her with sensuous appreciation.

'Don't panic,' he warned in that dark, velvet voice. 'I thought we were being robbed.'

Abigail didn't like the intimate sound of 'we' and she turned quickly away, not knowing what to do when she realised that she was standing there staring at him and her only covering was her silky white panties. She had been forced to take off her slip to try on some of the low-cut gowns and she hadn't bothered to put it back on again.

'Please go out and shut the door, Logan,' she choked, but he made no move to leave.

'I know what you look like, Abbie,' he reminded her softly. 'I know every inch of you. I know the feel of your silken skin, the way your black hair flows over those soft shoulders and down your back. I've never forgotten and you look the same. You'll feel the same if I touch you.'

'Please, Logan!' she begged shakily. She was trembling with a mixture of alarm and unexpected excitement. There had been no other man in her life either before or since Logan and she was afraid of the instant reaction of her body to the dark sound of his voice, terrified at the way his words seemed to slide into her emotions like a slow caress.

'I'm not touching you at all, Abbie,' he reminded her, his voice deepening huskily. 'Words can't hurt you.'

She made a wild grab for a dress, holding it up in front of her although she was still turned away from him, but he was behind her before she could speak again.

'Don't hide,' he said thickly. 'It's too late to hide. I've already seen you. I told you when I brought you here from the hospital that you had to undress yourself because I knew how I would feel.' His breath was warm against her shoulder and his hand ran along her trembling flesh and under the black fall of her hair. 'Do you think I'm made of stone, Abbie?'

'I—I didn't know you were here,' she gasped desperately. 'I didn't think you would come.'

'I was passing and I saw your car,' he murmured darkly, his hands beginning to mould her shoulders suggestively. 'I wondered what you were up to. I never expected to find you like this.'

'I came to—to get some clothes,' she managed breathlessly. 'I was trying them on.' Logan laughed softly, his lips coming to trail along her shoulder as he bent his head.

'Keep talking, Abbie,' he advised in a low voice. 'It's safer.'

'I'm going!' She stiffened, fighting the drugging sound of his voice, the tempting pressure of his fingers. She dared not stay like this. Everything inside her was melting towards him. She tried to move away and he reached for the dress she still held before her in a forlorn attempt at protection. He dropped it on the floor and his hands slid round her waist as he pulled her back against the hard warmth of his body.

'Don't,' he ordered huskily. 'You said that to me once. "Don't leave me, Logan." You also said, "for ever."'

His hands moved upwards to cover her breasts and his head bent to kiss the side of her neck. 'I still want you, Abigail. I warned you.'

'It's not fair!' She sobbed out the words and he tilted her head back, his caressing hands moving over her curves, making her treacherous body begin to yield against him.

'Nothing is fair,' he agreed deeply. 'I found that out a long time ago.' His lips moved over her cheeks and down to the curve of her jaw. 'This has nothing to do with fairness. This is desire and it's burning you too, sweet Abigail. You want me.'

Outside, the rain was pouring; the bedroom was only softly lit by the one lamp she had switched on as she'd come in. It was like another world, a place out of time, only dreamed of, and Abigail sank into the temptation of Logan's insistent hands and sensual words. For so long she had missed his touch and she gave a low murmur of anguish. When he turned her she moved submissively against him, her breath a sob of pleasure as he caught her close and brought his mouth down on hers.

His hands ran over her as his lips held her captive and she moved with mounting pleasure beneath the ardent pressure of his fingers. Everything inside her was aroused, hungry, and the sensual warmth of his breath when he lifted his head to place hot kisses on her neck was like a well-remembered flame.

Her arms wound around his neck and she simply gave in to the burning hunger that had never really left her. The thought of Logan that she had kept hidden in her mind for four years was now wildly alive and all other thoughts fled. It was like being held for the first time, the excitement threatening to make her faint.

'Logan!' she sobbed out his name and his arms clasped her tightly as he lifted her and lowered her to the bed, his hand sweeping the beautiful garments to the floor.

'I know,' he breathed thickly. 'It hurts, Abigail, doesn't it? It's like a hot knife inside.' He hovered over her, discarding his jacket, his shirt pulled impatiently over his head as he almost tore off his tie. 'Does Wingate know what you like as much as I do? Can he make you drift to the very edge of consciousness in his arms?'

He came down on top of her before she could protest, before she could even think of denying her relationship with Brian. It was too late then. Her body was already yearning, sensitised to the point of despair by the touch of his skin against hers.

'Abigail.' He clasped her face in his hands as he rested on strong forearms, his weight only lightly on the flat smoothness of her stomach. 'You know I won't stop now, don't you? You know I can't.'

She couldn't answer. Her lips were trembling and her only way of showing her acquiescence was to touch his face with delicate fingers as her eyes, wide and green, looked into his.

'Dear heavens! he muttered hoarsely. 'You've no idea how you look, have you? You've never known how much I want you, how obsessed I am with this silken body.'

His lips covered hers almost violently and she made no move at all to resist him. Her own lips opened willingly and she moved against him softly and insistently as he slid out of the rest of his clothes without even moving his mouth from hers.

She felt his hands on her, sliding away the only covering she had, and then their bodies were touching completely for the first time in the long four years.

'Logan!' She cried his name wildly and heard his dark, sensuous laughter.

'I'm here, my lovely,' he said with an almost ferocious satisfaction. 'I know that frantic cry. I remember, Abigail.'

After that there was no more talking. There was just the delirious rapture of Logan's touch, his deep, penetrating kisses and the frenzied movements of her own body as she strained to be even closer. The demanding murmurs of her own voice were still as familiar to her own ears as they were to Logan and his hands restrained her as his lips coaxed and teased.

'Now, my wild little Abbie,' he whispered thickly when she was sobbing his name and running her fingers madly through his thick hair. 'Tell me.'

'I want you.' She gasped out the words that he had always demanded, her hands clutching him to her, and she heard his low, masculine growl of satisfaction. She had heard it so many times before, his pleasure at her total commitment to him, and she sighed as her world shattered around her, light and colour mingling with velvet darkness as, after so long, Logan held her tightly and took her into another dimension that drove everything else away. Abigail rocked on the edge of consciousness, drowning in sensation, only the tight clasp of Logan's arms keeping her in the world.

'Shh,' he whispered, his voice like a light in the engulfing darkness. 'It's all right. I'm here. Shh.' He stroked back her hair with gentle hands and it was the well-remembered sound of the soothing words that broke the spell holding her in another place. She fell to earth, trembling violently, and Logan tucked her close to him, wrapping his arms around her.

'Shh,' he said softly. 'You've not changed, have you? You always felt too much, Abigail. Holding you to the earth was always a fight. What would happen if I let you go, do you think? Where would that eager body, that wildly soaring mind take you? I never dared take the chance of finding out.'

He held her silently until the violent spasm of trembling quietened and cold, numbing reality came back. Sheer, stark grief engulfed her then. What had she done? What had she let happen? Logan loved her no more now than he had ever done. The loving had all been hers from the first. He wanted her and nothing more.

She felt betrayed, not by him but by herself; all her principles had been abandoned, her integrity shattered. She had held herself aloof, planning to make a new life when this was over, and the moment he had touched her she had collapsed into his arms.

Abigail turned away from him, struggling to sit up and reaching for her clothes.

'You want me to shower with you?' Logan asked lazily, and she stiffened at the seductive sound of his question.

'Stop it!' she bit out, anger at herself a bitter taste in her throat.

'I always did,' he reminded her. He trailed one indolent finger down her spine, making her shiver and pull away. 'You tell lies, Abigail. Your father tells lies and so do you. It must run in the family.'

'I don't ever—!' Abigail began as her head spun round, her eyes flashing green sparks at him.

'You do,' he interrupted evenly. 'Poor Wingate. I savaged him for no reason at all. Nobody has touched you since you left my arms four years ago.'

'Don't fool yourself.' She turned away, frantically searching for her clothes, terribly aware that Logan still lay there, relaxed and magnificent, a mocking smile on his lips.

'I'm not fooling myself,' he assured her quietly. 'Abigail, I know your body as I know my own. It was always mine and it still is.'

'I suppose you think that little trick was clever,' she snapped, her flushed face turned away from him.

'There was no trick, Abigail,' he pointed out in amusement. 'You came to me gladly. I gave as much as you gave.'

No, she thought in anguish. He gave nothing. He only had desire.

'Really?' Now fully dressed, she stood and turned to him, her face composed. 'Well, it backfired. I don't need these clothes now because I'm not going with you. And,' she added when his grey eyes simply looked at her with wry amusement, 'you can threaten all you want to. My father will be strong enough to take over when he comes home from hospital and I'll be going to another job.'

Logan didn't stir. He was lying back with an arm behind his head, one strong leg raised comfortably, and she had to force herself to ignore the sheer masculine beauty. His lips twisted in a sardonic smile as he looked at her.

'Your father will have nothing to take control of,' he assured her. 'The moment I'm certain that this childish defiance is real, I'll reactivate everything. At the moment, my bankers are servicing your debts, keeping your bank in a state of hopeful euphoria. If I pull the plug there will be an unseemly rush to chop up the Madden Corporation. I have no feeling of generosity towards Kent Madden and just because I've taken your body I do not feel obliged to give you the firm. You enjoyed it as much as I did, wanted it as much as I did. The bargain stands or the firm falls.'

He looked at her with taunting amusement and she stared at him wildly.

'Servicing our debts? You can't be!'

'You're unworldly, Abigail,' he mocked, laughter touching his mouth. 'Why do you think the bank and everyone else held off? Do you imagine I'm so powerful that I held up my hand and said, Stop?'

In effect she had and the truth of that was on her face. His smile widened into a grin and he rolled over, reaching for his own clothes.

'Oh, Abbie,' he teased gently, 'if I were half as powerful as you seem to think, I'd rule the world.'

'I'll have to go with you, won't I?' she muttered miserably, and he turned to face her, tucking his shirt into his trousers, seeing the forlorn look on her face.

'I'm afraid so,' he commiserated. 'Maybe after today you'll be able to play the part better.'

'It will never happen again!' she assured him sharply, and his intent gaze narrowed on her downcast face.

'Never is a long time. When the time comes, you'll forget all about never.'

She flushed at his words and spun round to leave but his voice stopped her before she had taken two steps.

'Your clothes, Abigail. I would hate it if your ordeal had all been for nothing.' He was taunting her again. He knew that it had not and never had been an ordeal. The only ordeal about it was coming back to earth, losing him. She began gathering her clothes and he went to the little safe set in the wall behind a beautiful Degas print. He took out her jewellery case and put it on the bed.

'You'll need some of these,' he informed her quietly. 'There'll be one or two social evenings and you need jewellery.' He held up a necklace glittering with emeralds. 'Take this. It was always my favourite. It matches your eyes.'

She almost snatched it from him and stuffed it into her bag with several other pieces. He had bought it for her as a wedding gift and she had loved it. But then, she had loved him too. It was part of a past she would discard as soon as this was over.

She turned away, a feeling of desolation washing over her. She still loved him and there was no chance of denying it. If he reached for her now she would fall into his arms. It was something he would never know and she hurried to the door, leaving the flat, slamming the outer door behind her.

The rain had stopped and Abigail packed her clothes into the car, being very careful not even to glance at the flat as she left. If he was watching her she would not give him the satisfaction of knowing how great was his victory. Her body ached and deep inside excitement still throbbed slowly. The need to be with Logan was growing and his knowing grey eyes had almost certainly assessed that. She would have to be very careful on this trip.

New York was hot. The flight had been exhausting too because even though they had come first class Abigail had been tense and miserable all the time. Now, as they were dropped at the hotel where they would spend the night, she felt as if her legs would give way beneath her.

'Have a meal in your room and then go to bed,' Logan advised her after a close look at her pale face. 'The only reason we're here is because I have a meeting tonight, otherwise we would have gone straight to our destination. It was perhaps a good idea after all, though; you look worn out.'

'I'm tired,' Abigail conceded. Being with him on the flight had been difficult because she was still crushed by the way she had given in. She recognised that she was feeling both guilty and disgusted with herself but if Logan realised he gave no sign of his knowledge.

In fact, he had spoken very little. He was not icy, simply indifferent. The other afternoon might just as well have been a figment of her imagination. It had had no effect at all on Logan, while she felt devastated.

'I'll get something sent up to you,' he murmured after coming to her room for a swift glance of inspection. 'If you need anything, I'm next door, although I'll be out within the hour and not back until late.'

He just nodded to her and left, closing the door firmly. It was as if she were his secretary. His cool politeness was an astonishing lesson in good manners and she sat on the bed wearily and stared at the door even after it had been closed.

If she had ever had any doubts about him then they were completely gone now. Logan was an aloof stranger; his lapse into passion had been merely a masculine need. She felt used and abandoned.

Abigail had a shower and when she came back into the bedroom there was a tray neatly placed on her table. Under the silver covers were dainty delicacies that would have tempted even the most exhausted of people. Logan always knew what to do in any situation. There was a note on the tray too. The words had been written by some unknown hand. 'Compliments of Mr Steele.'

She grimaced. How had he signed them in to the hotel, to their separate rooms? Was she put down as Mrs Steele? They must be thought an odd couple. Separate sleeping

arrangements and her supper sent with compliments.
'Send supper up to my wife, with my compliments.' It
would have been amusing if it had not made her feel
lonely. Her feelings swayed between despair and regret
and she dreaded tomorrow.

Playing his wife would be an ordeal. She would have
to be close. He would touch her. Without that the game
would be up and it couldn't be. She hoped this man,
whoever he was, expected no show of affection, merely
immaculate manners. Logan could satisfy that re-
quirement very well. Why had he needed her here? Why
couldn't he have taken a photograph of her to show off
proudly and told them she was ill?

It was cruel, his way of showing that he had a death-
grip on the firm her father lived for. She nibbled at her
supper and before long crept into bed. Somewhere out
there in this teeming city, Logan would be engaged in
the thing he loved most—power games. It was all he
loved. He didn't love her and she wondered if he loved
Fenella Mitchell. Perhaps not. If he had done, he would
have demanded a divorce ages ago.

She was being stupid, her tired mind grasping at fan-
tasies. She turned on her side, determined to sleep. At
least in sleep she could escape from the worry of the
next days—or weeks. Logan hadn't said. She was totally
dependent on him. They all were—her father, Rose,
Martha, the loyal people at the firm. Everything relied
on her and as usual the weight hung around her heart
and refused to move.

They arrived in California the next afternoon and Abigail
was much recovered. She looked better than Logan because, for the first time ever, she saw lines of strain on
the handsome face. She had no idea how late he had

been the previous evening but the superb physical power was looking slightly drained today.

A long white car met them at the airport and Abigail's hopes brightened as she saw the man who waited for them.

'Here he is,' Logan said quietly, and then she was being introduced to the man who disliked any idea of mistresses and divorce. He was well past middle age, white-haired but very healthy-looking—too young to retire, in Abigail's opinion. He had a nice open smile too. He shook hands heartily with Logan and beamed at Abigail.

'My wife, Abigail,' Logan said, taking her hand. 'Abbie, this is Grant Cassidy.' He had no time to say any more because Grant Cassidy gave her a big hug.

'The most beautiful thing I've ever seen,' he said. 'You must excuse my enthusiasm, little lady, but I've heard all about you from Logan. I thought he was exaggerating but he wasn't.'

Abigail managed a bright smile but her mind was somewhat stunned. In the first place she was not little, although Logan towered over her and this man was like a well-meaning bear. That Logan had told him about her brought some credibility to the situation. She could see that they knew each other and if he had left her in England it would have looked suspicious.

'Knew his grandpa *and* his uncle Greg,' Grant Cassidy confided to her, tucking her arm in his and leading her to the car. 'Never managed to get him down here to my place, though. This is a big day.' He looked round impatiently and then added apologetically, 'Waiting for Pete. He'll be here in a second.'

He chatted to Logan, and Abigail was content to wait at the side of the huge car. After flying for so long it was a relief to stand and stretch her legs. She wasn't really paying much attention to the conversation so she was startled into looking up when Grant Cassidy suddenly said, 'He's here. Come and meet this delightful creature, Pete.'

And then Abigail found herself facing a man whose presence alarmed her immediately.

'This is Logan's wife.' Grant introduced her enthusiastically. 'I've told you about Logan Steele, and this is his wife, Abigail.'

'Well, hello, Abigail.' She found her hand taken and kept too long and she looked up into two eyes that held her mesmerised. Beside her she felt Logan stiffen with annoyance and she could understand why. Even the way he had said her name had been a sort of disrespectful intimacy.

'This is my son, Pete,' Grant Cassidy informed them, and she found herself comparing the wholesome appearance of Grant and the smooth, speculating looks of his son. She almost snatched her hand away but the eyes still watched her steadily. They were dark—too dark— with a dull gleam at the back of them. He almost made her shudder openly.

He was possibly twenty-eight or nine, too slick in his appearance, his pale hair smoothed back against a good-looking bronzed face. She had the awful feeling that he was waiting to pounce and she wondered how any girl could be attracted to him. He was insolently sure of himself, his gaze filled with cold sexual appraisal. He had shocked her into immobility and Abigail found herself unable to step back in spite of her distaste. His dark eyes never left hers and they were almost hypnotic. He had the eyes of a cobra.

CHAPTER SEVEN

THEY were dropped at their hotel, and after seeing Pete Cassidy Abigail was more than delighted that they were not staying at the Cassidy home. The younger Cassidy was someone she must avoid at all costs. She assumed that he gave his undivided, insolent attention to every woman he met but she found it revolting. Just meeting him had been a disturbing experience. Living under the same roof would have been impossible, especially as she would have had to keep her temper because of Logan's business deal.

'Did Grant Cassidy book us in here?' she asked when the car had left and they were standing in the foyer of the low white hotel with its Spanish arches and wrought-iron balconies.

'No, I did,' Logan said shortly.

He was still stiffly angry after their encounter with Grant's son and as they followed the porter to the stairs in silence Abigail didn't venture into conversation again. She was too busy worrying about the sleeping arrangements. Now they were here on the home territory of the man who expected marital bliss. Would they have to have a double room in case Grant found out? The thought made her nervous and Logan glanced at her in irritation when she looked at him warily.

'These are your rooms,' the porter said, opening two doors. 'There's a connecting balcony.'

'Splendid,' Logan growled irascibly. 'I trust it does not connect with anyone else.'

'You're completely private here, sir.'

Abigail thought the porter gave them an odd look but Logan ignored such things. He ordered tea and they were left alone, their luggage placed neatly by the bed, while Abigail stood beside it as if she were also labelled with their air-flight number.

'Whichever room you want,' Logan said in a detached voice after one more disparaging glance at her, and Abigail shrugged.

'They both seem to be the same. It doesn't matter.'

Logan nodded and picked up his own luggage, going through the connecting door and leaving her to it, and she gave a resigned sigh as she opened her cases. If this was how he was going to behave, then Grant Cassidy might well change his mind about marriage. She wondered what Mrs Cassidy was like and once again shuddered as she thought of their son.

The waiter came and served tea on the balcony and Abigail abandoned her task to go outside and sit in the last of the sunshine. This was a small hotel. It didn't even have a lift because it was spread in all directions across truly beautiful gardens. The rooftops were of different heights, red-tiled against the white of the walls, and many of the rooms seemed to be at ground level. Their rooms, though, were obviously special. They were at the very centre of the hotel, in a sort of tower that gave balance to the whole place. There was a lovely view of the gardens and the curved balcony looked out to sea.

It was rather like a hacienda and Abigail stood waiting for Logan to join her, her eyes feasting on the Spanish flavour of the place and the wide expanse of sandy beach that led down to a tranquil blue-green sea.

'It's wonderful!' She turned with shining eyes as Logan came through to the balcony and his gaze flashed over her face, his mouth twisting wryly.

'It was recommended by someone who travels here often,' he murmured. He sat at the white wrought-iron table and began to pour the tea before she could even offer, and Abigail's enjoyment was somewhat curbed. She recognised the look he had given her. She was being enthusiastic again, with no sophistication, just as she had been when he had taken her on a boat on the Thames five years ago.

She sat down silently, nodding her thanks when Logan passed her tea across. So many things he did threw her headlong into the past and now she felt subdued and it showed on her face.

'Tonight Grant Cassidy and his wife are dining here with us,' Logan announced, and Abigail looked up quickly.

'Pete Cassidy?' she asked sharply, and Logan's lips tightened.

'I didn't enquire. I simply looked exclusively at Grant. The hope that the younger Cassidy would be more interested in a nightclub was uppermost in my mind.'

Distaste showed on Abigail's face.

'He's got eyes like a snake—a cobra.'

'I've heard that cobras have beautiful eyes,' Logan muttered as he drank his tea, and she looked disgusted.

'Not when the eyes belong to a person. He makes me shudder.'

'I can't say he fills me with delight and admiration,' Logan agreed. He moved his chair back and sat with one leg resting on his knee. 'He looks like trouble.'

'If we ignore him, he may go away,' Abigail pointed out hopefully, and Logan raised one black brow.

'I find it difficult to ignore a pest. Steer clear of him.' It was a stern order and Abigail looked at him with annoyance.

'It would be nice to know I could slap his face and tell him to go away,' she retorted. 'Unfortunately that would not endear you to his father and the deal would fall through.'

'You put up with *nothing*!' Logan pinned her with crystal eyes, temper edging his lips. 'Not one thing. He acts and you react! Do you hear me, Abigail?'

'I'm not deaf,' she said quickly, looking round anxiously. Logan had raised his voice and she was glad to find that there was not a soul in sight.

'Anyway,' Logan continued in a more reasonable tone, 'you'll be with me. I told Grant that this was a second honeymoon and he's hugging himself with glee. That being the case, he'll expect to see us in intimate conversation and not more than one inch apart. I can look after you with no worries about the younger Cassidy.'

Abigail managed to look at him coolly, quelling the sudden leaping of her pulse.

'What a good job Grant Cassidy doesn't know about the two adjoining rooms,' she said tartly and without much thought, her main idea being to stifle her instant flustered reaction with instant speech. 'When you send my supper up with your compliments he'll be quite taken aback!'

Logan grinned widely, his grey eyes dancing over her flushed face.

'It amused me,' he confessed. 'It startled the man at the reception desk. I was laughing all evening.'

Abigail frowned at him. Not much chance of that. In New York he had been wheeling and dealing. When

Logan went into action there wasn't a smile in sight. He was like a tiger, hunting.

'If you get lonely,' he continued in a low murmur, 'you can always drift along the balcony to me.'

'I'd rather drift over the balcony rail,' Abigail snapped, getting to her feet to glare down at him before walking to her own French window.

'You're telling lies again,' Logan taunted softly, his eyes following her graceful figure. 'Try to resist it. It's a hard habit to break when it runs in the family.'

She walked out of his sight, her soft lips drooping as soon as he couldn't see. He never forgot, never missed a trick, never missed a chance to drive home the guilt, and now she was not so sure of her father's innocence. She had seen for herself how callous and devious he could be and she had never had any doubt about Logan's cruel truthfulness.

Once again her mind went over his reason for helping them. He had gone to a good deal of trouble over several years to get them in his clutches. Now he had simply opened his tightening grasp and steadied the sinking ship.

And all because of one business transaction in America? If she hadn't been here with him she would not have believed it; in fact, at the back of her mind she didn't really believe it now. Almost daily since he had made his offer she had been dreading finding out that it was one more ploy to overthrow her father and take his revenge.

She had no choice but to go along with it, whatever his final plans were, and being with him brought its own problems because she still loved him and he only had to lift a finger to call her to his side; whatever else happened, she must not let him know that.

Dinner was pleasant because Pete Cassidy did not come after all. Grant's wife was a rather plain woman with hair dyed an astonishingly dull black. It was so obviously dyed that it drew Abigail's eyes like a magnet and she had to be very stern with herself in order to ignore it. Left to itself, it would probably have been grey, and Mrs Cassidy would have looked much better like that.

'Oh, honey, look!' she exclaimed to Grant as she met Abigail. 'A real brunette. Look at the blue-black shine. You just can't get that colour.'

Grant grinned at Abigail when she looked flustered and didn't know what to say.

'Ivy changes her hair colour as often as she changes her mind,' he chuckled. 'This week she's a brunette. It was red the week before.'

'Ash-blonde!' Ivy Cassidy corrected him, giving him a sharp dig in the ribs. 'Red was last month.'

'I lose track,' he laughed, and Abigail's embarrassment faded at this open discussion. She laughed too. Logan looked somewhat astounded but he covered his astonishment by leading them in to dinner—a candlelit meal on a wide veranda overlooking the sea.

A round table had been set for them, the crystal glittering in the light from the flickering candles. There were white roses in the centre of the table and in the shelter of the veranda, with its trailing greenery and brightly coloured potted plants, it looked beautiful.

'This is really romantic,' Ivy cooed, and Grant smiled knowingly at her.

'Second honeymoon,' he confided in a loud whisper. 'We have to remember to leave at a respectable time.'

Abigail's face flushed like a wild rose and Logan, helping her to her chair, lingered behind her, his hands coming to her shoulders seductively.

'We've got all the time in the world,' he told them easily. 'The second honeymoon started before we even left England.'

It sent Abigail's mind spinning back to the flat, back to the lamplit bedroom, and she had to struggle hard not to flinch under his taunting hands. What was she expected to do—look coy? Apparently her romantically flushed cheeks were enough to satisfy Logan because he sat opposite her with a very complacent look on his handsome face. Ivy and Grant Cassidy beamed at them both.

No business was discussed. Grant seemed to want to talk about the old days—about Logan's grandfather and his uncle. She learned a lot about Logan—things she had not known before. He had come to America to go to Harvard and he'd simply stayed on, working with his grandfather and uncle, learning in the fast, hard world of American business.

'They were quick on their feet in those days,' Grant reminisced. 'Logan's grandpa was a whirlwind, right to the end. His uncle Greg was the same. There wasn't much that those two didn't know between them. You had to be up real early in the morning to even begin to compete.'

No wonder Logan was in a towering league of his own, Abigail thought. Apparently he had learned from two experts, lived with them and worked with them. It was not surprising that the Madden Corporation had been slowly squeezed almost out of existence.

'I couldn't believe it when your uncle Greg was killed in that car crash soon after your grandpa died. What a tragedy.' He glanced at Logan speculatively. 'Everybody expected you to stay here and carry on, seeing that everything came to you. It was a real shock when you went back to England and left things to managers.'

'My roots are there,' Logan said briefly. 'I never had any real intention of staying in the States.'

'Sure,' Grant murmured. 'Couldn't be expected, I suppose, with your folks in England. Your dad married an English girl, after all. I lost track of him after that. How is he?'

'He died.'

Logan said nothing more and Grant looked shocked. He murmured his regrets and Abigail felt the shock too, deep inside. It wasn't that she hadn't known. When they'd been together, Logan had never once mentioned his parents, and the first she had known of them was what he'd told her at the office on the day she had fainted. Martha had told her too, so the shock was not that. The fact was not new to her. It was the cold, bitter way in which Logan said it that brought shock.

The chill came racing back round her heart. He had not forgiven, not forgotten and with Logan that meant only one thing—revenge.

Whatever calculating game he was playing now, she knew without doubt that the helping hand he had held out to the firm was of cold iron clothed in velvet. She was here, risking everything for that helping hand, but the vendetta continued and it would continue until her father was destroyed.

Logan was playing some deep, unfathomable game with them. Making love to her at the flat might or might not have been part of it. Not that it mattered. He had won there too and she knew that there would be no bright and hopeful future. Their escape did not figure in Logan's plans and so there would be no escape at all.

Grant didn't ask about Logan's mother but Abigail was on edge, waiting for the question to come. Logan's words were ringing in her head—the words he had used when she had gone to his office to capitulate. 'Remind him about John Steele and his wife, Kathleen.' Then she had been outraged, disbelieving, but now there was a growing doubt, and the thought of her father being responsible for two deaths horrified her.

Afterwards, when Grant and Ivy left, Abigail went with Logan to see their guests off. It was a beautiful night. There was a moon riding high in a dark blue sky, the sound of the ocean and the frothy surf bubbling on the sand.

Abigail stood for a moment as the car pulled away, her eyes lingering on the scene, and Logan watched her, his gaze roaming over her slender shape in her ivory-coloured dress—a sharp contrast to her shimmering black hair.

'Want to walk on the beach?' he enquired quietly.

She did but she was nervous. This time her nerves were not there because she did not trust herself with Logan. She was anxious about his attitude when he had told Grant and Ivy about his father's death. She was desperate to find out the truth but terrified to ask.

'I would, really,' she said in a hesitant voice. 'You—you don't have to come, though; I can—'

'Don't annoy me, Abigail,' he cut in coldly, taking her arm and leading her across the garden to the beach path. 'The fact that you've been looking at me in dismay all evening has not escaped my attention.'

'I haven't!' Abigail protested, stopping to look up at him. In the moonlight and with the hotel lights now left behind, he looked tall and forbidding. The eyes he turned on her flashed silver with the reflection of the moon and she felt her breath almost stop at the look on his face.

'I told you that I never lie,' he grated. 'The news of my father's death did not come as any surprise to you. You *know* he died. So why the look of horror, Abigail? Were you afraid I would go on to recount just how and why he died? What did you imagine I would say— And Abigail's father brought his death about? Were you waiting for that, cringing with anticipation?'

'No! I never even thought of it!' she exclaimed. She pulled her arm from his grasp and walked away but he was behind her immediately, his anger rising even more.

'Don't walk away from me!' he ordered harshly. 'If you think I'm letting you wander alone on the beach you can forget it.' He dropped into step beside her and she shook her head with every sign of despair.

'I didn't *want* to walk alone on the beach and I didn't think you would even mention my father. Whatever happens, I seem to get the blame. Whatever happens, the responsibility is handed to me.' She bit her lip, too choked up inside to say any more, and Logan gave a low growl of annoyance as he grasped her shoulders and swung her round to face him.

'When have I ever given you responsibility?' he queried stormily. 'I protected you, cared for you, practically carried you around when we were together. Look at me!' he finished angrily.

She continued to look down and he tilted her face up impatiently, his anger dying as the moonlight lightened her pale face and shimmering eyes.

'You little idiot,' he muttered, pulling her forward until his arms enclosed her. 'I never learn, do I? I should just pick you up and carry you off somewhere.'

She felt warm against him; his hands slowly caressed her back and his head bent to hers until his lips could trail across the tender line of her jaw.

'I wasn't looking anxious because of—because of the thought that you might mention my father,' she told him quietly, but she could tell that he was not really listening. Instead he was breathing in the scent of her, his arms tightening. 'Logan,' she prompted when he didn't reply.

'Hmm?' His voice sounded deep, almost drowsy and she raised her face to look at him, grasping the moment.

'I didn't think you would speak about my father,' she insisted quietly. 'I'm learning more about him every day. Once I was certain but now—I don't know.'

Logan dropped his arms, letting her go, walking along the beach, and she had to walk with him.

'I'll never tell you anything about it, Abigail,' he said tightly. 'I didn't tell you before and I'm not telling you now. If you're expecting the details from me you'll be waiting for ever.'

'I'm not expecting anything,' she assured him, almost in a whisper, and Logan gave a short, harsh laugh.

'No, you never did. Even now you imagine that you have no rights. You take everything he hands out and come up for more, don't you?'

'And everything you hand out too,' Abigail reminded him bitterly. 'If I staunchly defended my rights, I wouldn't be here now.'

'Where would you be—with Wingate?' He spun round and glared at her and that just about finished it off. Abigail turned to march back to the hotel, her angry departure somewhat spoiled when her high heels sank into soft sand as she stepped out a little too briskly.

She muttered crossly, bending to take off her sandals, but she was scooped up into two strong arms and Logan proceeded to carry her back with no effort.

'Put me down!' She struggled uselessly, her dignity ruined, and he didn't even look at her.

'Shut up, Abbie,' he murmured softly. 'I'll just pretend that you're still nineteen and everything will be all right. You haven't really progressed much. Even the dresses still fit you. You glow with the same old look of innocence and purity. You certainly don't look as if you've ever been a wife. Grant probably thinks I kidnapped you from a convent.'

She didn't quite know what to make of that but out of the corner of her eye she could see Logan's wide grin back in place and she was grateful for that at least.

Abigail slept deeply that night, the soft breeze from the balcony blowing the gauzy curtains and soothing her. It was later than usual when she awoke next morning and she hurried to get up, wondering if Logan had already had breakfast. When she ventured onto the balcony there was no sign of him, no noise from his room and she looked over the rail as she heard a car approaching the hotel.

She soon found out where Logan was because he came through the front door of the hotel and walked to the car to greet the newcomer. Abigail drew back, thinking it might be Grant Cassidy and not wanting to be seen undressed. The voice was not masculine, though. It was a voice she had heard only once before but she knew it as she knew her own nightmares.

'Well, I'm here, darling, and utterly exhausted.'

'You look dazzling as ever,' Logan assured her in an amused voice. 'Quite obviously overnight flights suit you. You should take one often.'

'Only if you command my presence.'

Abigail looked over the rail, knowing what she would see, and she was not disappointed. Fenella Mitchell was walking back to the hotel, clinging to Logan's arm. He had her briefcase in his hand and behind them trailed a porter with her luggage.

'Thank goodness you're here,' Logan muttered as they came directly below Abigail. His deep voice carried even though he was speaking quietly and Abigail's heart began to break all over again.

She had been through this once and she couldn't face it again, even though this time she was here acting out a lie. Logan had summoned his mistress to his side because he couldn't manage without her and she would be with him on the other side of the connecting door, breakfasting with them, attending any social functions.

Abigail began to pack her cases, fighting a mixture of humiliation and rage. She would be out of here before lunchtime, even before she had eaten breakfast. Logan could not expect this. What had he said last night? He had never given her any responsibility. No, he had treated her like a fool and he was doing it all over again. No doubt it was part of the punishment he was handing out to her father. She was to be punished too, for being a Madden by birth.

Logan walked in a few minutes later and the pleased look on his face faded into anger as he saw her cases on the long luggage stool, her clothes on the bed ready to pack.

'What the hell are you doing?' he rasped, his eyes glittering with annoyance.

'Leaving,' Abigail said tightly. 'The game's up, the show is over. Tell Grant Cassidy that I ran off with the hotel manager.'

Logan advanced like a menacing jungle cat but she didn't back off; her green eyes were glittering too, as angry as his own.

'You'd better explain before I really lose my temper,' he warned, and she flared into rage, her eyes flashing sparks.

'What do you take me for?' she bit out furiously. 'I was blackmailed into coming here to play a part that sickens me and now you've summoned your mistress to join us. How do you propose to explain that to Grant— You've already met my wife, Grant, but this is Fenella. She's different—I can't manage without her?'

'Of course I can't manage without her!' Logan snapped. 'She's the company lawyer. I can't sign a damned thing without her.'

'Don't insult my intelligence!' Abigail stormed. '*We* have a company lawyer and he doesn't call the chairman "darling".'

'I see. You were leaning over the balcony, spying and listening.' Logan looked at her in a scathing manner and Abigail's temper rose accordingly.

'I went to look for you and you weren't there. I was out of sight because I wasn't dressed.'

'You're not dressed now,' Logan pointed out, and she ignored him, getting back to her task.

'I will be as soon as I've packed this case. Obviously you think I'm stupid—too stupid to react to this—this insult. Too stupid even to care for a child when we were married and too stupid to see through this subterfuge.'

'You're jealous,' Logan said with a good deal of satisfaction, his temper easing. 'If you're here because I blackmailed you, and I admit that I did, then why should you react so violently to Fenella's presence?' He took her shoulders, spinning her to face him. 'I've told you, Abigail, she's my lawyer. I need her here or she would not be here. This is a game you're in, to get the deal with Grant. She's here to add her signature when he agrees to the deal and she's here for no other reason.'

'Well, you can count me out of this game,' Abigail snapped, struggling under his hands, too angry and hurt to feel any sort of magic. 'I'm going home and nothing you can say will make me change my mind.'

Logan scooped her up into his arms, ignoring her struggles.

'I'm not going to say anything,' he assured her grimly. 'Talking is over. This is all you understand.'

He dropped her on the bed, trapping her when she tried to roll away, towering over her with sensuously teasing eyes.

'Don't touch me!' Abigail warned shakily, and his lips tilted in a cynical smile of amusement, his eyes holding hers unwaveringly.

'You keep reminding me that you wanted a baby,' he murmured as he pulled off his tie and began to unbutton his shirt. 'I've changed my mind, Abbie. You can have a baby. Maybe it will give you a small amount of sense and keep you out of mischief.'

'No!' She tried to struggle up but he knelt above her, watching her with amused eyes that began to take on the slow-burning glaze of desire.

'Yes, Abbie,' he said softly. 'You're jealous. How else am I going to prove that Fenella means nothing to me? She's here right now but it's you I want. In about one second you'll be begging me to love you.'

'You don't love me!' The cry was torn from her and he came down to her, gathering her to him, his lips tracing her neck and shoulders as he pushed aside the straps of her nightdress.

'Is that what you want me to say?' he asked thickly. 'All right. I love you. Does that make it any better, Abbie? Does that ease your mind and make that jealousy go away? Does that make Fenella into a lawyer and nothing else?'

'No!' she cried, struggling to move away from his coaxing lips. 'She's your mistress. She always has been. She's like you—hard, unfeeling, ruthless.'

'You never grew up after all,' he breathed, seeking her lips and holding her tossing head to make it still beneath his searching mouth. 'It doesn't much matter. I still go crazy when you're close to me. I still watch the way you walk and want to reach out and get you.' He buried his face against her breasts, breathing in her perfume. 'You smell like a flower,' he whispered huskily. 'A morning rose, delicate and dewy. You always did. You've always haunted my dreams.'

His lips closed over hers and she moaned softly, her fight gone, her limbs relaxing, opening to welcome him without any message from her mind. Her arms wound around his neck and he lifted his lips from hers, his teeth gently biting her lower lip.

'Tell me,' he demanded, breathing the words into her mouth. 'Tell me, Abbie.'

'I want you,' she said imploringly and he stroked her nightie away, his hands caressing her heated skin

'And I want you,' he said thickly. 'There's never a moment when I don't want you, never a moment since the first time I saw you in that red sweater and black shirt, your hair flowing over your shoulders and your eyes the most beautiful eyes I've ever seen.'

'But you never loved me,' she lamented, her hands on his face, her lips eagerly searching for his.

'Does it matter?' he muttered, his breathing fast and ragged. 'What do you care? You'll go into that spinning, far-off place you fly to and you'll never know how I feel, will you? One day, I'll let you go there completely, but not now, Abbie. Now you'll stay with me and come back with me.'

He rolled away to undress and she followed, her arms clinging to him, her lips searching for his, and when he came back to her they were already too lost in excitement to wait. At the back of her mind she mourned, wept, but she could never fight Logan. She wanted to be part of him—she always had wanted to be part of him, wanted to melt into him and stay there—so she wrapped herself around him, going where he led until the world exploded around them and she flew off into an expanding universe.

He called her back, held her close and the usual storm of trembling engulfed her as she whimpered gently against Logan's shoulder as he held her fast.

'Oh, Abbie!' he whispered hoarsely. 'What am I going to do with you? It's like a long, melancholy battle in the dark—no end, no hope.'

She knew that and she buried her face against him until the trembling slowed and the room looked light again. She was lifeless, just a part of him, and there was no joy in her mind.

'Come on.' Logan lifted her into his arms and walked to the shower and this time she simply acquiesced, standing subdued and obedient while he showered them both. Now she couldn't go. She was lost, a mere extension of Logan, a bewildered victim in a struggle to the end. He bent his head and kissed her cold lips and for a second her own despair seemed to show on his face.

She stayed in the bathroom to get dry and when she came out, a white bathrobe tied around her, Logan was already dressed. Her clothes were gone too and she knew that he had put them all back in the wardrobe.

'I've ordered breakfast up here for you,' he said quietly. 'It should be obvious to you that I have to have breakfast with Fenella. We have things to discuss and, apart from the fact that you would be bored, I'm not asking you to come and eat with us and get upset. You obviously distrust me.'

Abigail didn't answer. She sat at the dressing table and began to dry her hair, her eyes avoiding him as she prayed that he would just go and let her recover in her own way and by herself.

'I can't keep you out of it all the time, Abigail,' he pointed out, coming to stand behind her and watching her in the wide mirror. 'We're invited to dinner at Grant's club tonight, as you know. She's going to be there.'

She looked up at him then, meeting his eyes in the reflection of the glass. He looked sombre. There was none of the amused satisfaction that he had shown after their lovemaking at the flat and she quickly looked away. She didn't understand him; maybe she never had.

'I expect I'll cope,' she told him quietly, her slender hands wielding the brush, sweeping it through her shining hair.

A spasm of pain crossed his expression and his eyes roamed over her from her downcast face to the graceful movement of her hands and the blue-black shine of her hair.

'There'll be a lot of people there,' he reminded her almost apologetically. 'It's not going to be any intimate dinner party.'

'It doesn't matter,' Abigail said dully, and he shrugged, turning to leave.

'By the way,' he murmured as he moved to the door, 'I phoned the hospital this morning. I thought you might like to know how your father is. He's fine.'

It was so unexpected that she spun round, her wide eyes searching his face. Why had he done that? It astonished her. She couldn't work out his motives and she just stared at him in silence.

His grey eyes narrowed, icing over as his sombre looks vanished into anger.

'Don't even bother to ask!' he said coldly. 'I can see your mind working. I can see you asking yourself if I called the hospital hoping to find he'd had a relapse.'

She hadn't thought that at all and she looked at him steadily.

'Such a thing never entered my mind,' she assured him slowly, taking at least one chance to strike a blow for herself. 'Don't judge everyone by the devious workings of your own mind. Some of us have much more straight-forward and simple thoughts. I was just surprised. Thank you for phoning and thank you for telling me, and if you think that's just the sweet manners of a simpleton then you're probably right. I've proved this morning what a fool I am, otherwise I would be downstairs now, booking my flight back home.'

Abigail turned away and continued to dry her hair and for a moment Logan watched her, the annoyance easing from his face and the sombre look returning more strongly. She ignored him and after a second he simply turned and left, closing the door quietly behind him.

She stopped pretending then, her tight restraint leaving her, and the dryer rested on the glass top of the dressing table as her head fell forward to her hands and her mind gave itself up to grief. Not only did she love him still, she loved him more than ever.

She had not thought it possible to feel even more strongly about Logan than she had felt when she'd first known him but the years had added a yearning and a hunger that now threatened to destroy her. She was not nineteen now. There was no romantic haze to her dreams. She needed Logan as part of herself. He was essential to her very existence and this time when it was over she would not be able to face a new life bravely without him. Even her faith in her father was gone. This time there would be nothing but emptiness.

CHAPTER EIGHT

AFTER breakfast, Fenella went to have a rest, and therefore, she realised, avoiding her would be comparatively easy. Abigail had this unwanted information from the talkative waiter when he came to collect her tray. Logan had gone out. She had that news from the same source and she lingered in her room and on the balcony, her eyes on the sea, her mind frantically searching for comfort.

There was no comfort, though. She wasn't even angry any more and when another waiter came and told her that her husband wanted her to join him for lunch she went downstairs like an obedient shadow, no expression on her face at all because she could not show her grief and Logan was too astute to mistake grief for either anger or outrage.

It was a silent meal and she knew that he had asked her to join him merely for appearance's sake. Once again there was a dark, serious expression on his face and after the meal he made his excuses and left her. She didn't know whether he was going to Fenella or going to his own room but, whatever he was doing, she could not go upstairs and simply wait for the evening's ordeal to catch up with her.

She went to the beach and walked in the hot sunlight, the breeze blowing her hair around her and cooling her face. Memories tried to surface but she squashed them immediately, making her mind blank, seeing only the sky and sea, passing other people as if they did not exist.

Abigail felt as if she did not exist either. She was not even really worried about the dinner at Grant's club tonight. She felt too numb inside to be concerned about a face-to-face meeting with Fenella Mitchell.

When she came back into the hotel garden she glanced up at the balcony that connected her room to Logan's. He was there, standing quite still, watching her, but he gave no sign that he saw her. He simply looked distant, cool and unreachable.

He was still there when she reached her room and he came to the French window as she walked in from the corridor.

'Eight o'clock tonight,' he stated, simply looking at her, and she nodded her agreement, waiting for him to leave.

'Take care in the sun,' he muttered when she said nothing at all. 'It's hot, not what you're used to. If you're going to the beach to walk, wait for the sun to die down a little.'

'I didn't walk for long,' Abigail assured him, turning wearily away from his grey-eyed stare.

'You walked for an hour, back and forth,' he corrected her, and her head shot round as she faced him with annoyance.

'How do you know? Haven't you anything better to do with your time than spy on me? Did you think I would sneak off?'

'I was watching to see that you were safe,' he snapped, anger racing across his face. 'Or maybe I can't keep my eyes off you,' he snarled furiously. 'Eight o'clock, Abigail!'

He walked off, bristling with anger, and she threw herself on the bed. Perhaps she should have a rest too. She felt worn out. It was a long time to eight o'clock and by then she knew she would be strung up tightly. Sleep seemed to be a good way out of things.

Abigail awoke in good time to get ready and she started at once because she knew she would need every kind of defence she could muster for tonight. Why didn't Grant and Logan get on with this deal? Why hadn't they signed the papers already? Because Fenella had only just arrived, she reminded herself. Now there was nothing to stop them and after that her whole life with Logan was over.

She had a turquoise dress, one that she had bought not long ago to attend a dinner with Brian. In the event she hadn't gone because there had been yet another crisis at the office and as usual her own plans had had to be shelved.

When she was ready she put the dress on and she could see why she had bought it. The colour was perfect for her black hair. The dress was off the shoulder, molded to her slender shape, swirling out around her from the waist down, and it gave her a good deal of satisfaction to know that Logan had not bought this for her. All the same, he had bought the narrow diamond necklace she wore with the matching bracelet. They brought back painful memories but she kept them on all the same.

Studying herself in the mirror, she thought she looked too young even in this finery and on an extravagant impulse that she did not usually possess she rang Reception and asked if there was a hairdresser on the hotel staff. There was, and when eight o'clock came round Abigail was as sophisticated as she was ever going to be, her hair swept up and swirled in a loose cascade of curls around her head.

Logan had rung her room to say that he would meet her in the foyer, and she gathered her gauzy turquoise scarf and went down to join him. He had not been prepared to come and escort her apparently but it was no surprise, Fenella was going with them and she would not like being left to wait by herself.

The stairs opened out at the bottom to wide, shallow steps and as Abigail went down into the well-lit foyer she was the focus of many eyes. She was nervously aware of it, her anxiety making her pale, almost ethereal and when she dared to look up Logan was coming to meet her, his eyes intently on her, his face serious and still. The crystal grey glance swept over her, lingering on every curve of her body, studying her face and the swirling shine of her hair.

It made her heart flutter and then thud into an uncomfortable beat. She could see raw desire on his face and she was sure that anyone watching would see it too. If there had been love there she would have fallen at his feet but there was nothing but a blazing need that made his eyes flare like silver lightning.

'Where is she?' Abigail did not give him time to greet her. Instead her eyes darted round the foyer, looking for the woman who would outshine her in every way.

'She's already left,' Logan said tightly. 'Pete Cassidy came to escort us so I got rid of him. I sent Fenella ahead and said I would wait for you.'

'You let her go with him?' Abigail looked up at him in surprise and he gave a very grim smile as he heard her astonishment. It was obvious that she had expected him to stay close to Fenella, equally obvious that she still believed that Fenella was his mistress.

'She can take care of herself,' he said icily. 'Fenella doesn't need any sort of protection. The younger Cassidy recognised that on sight. He went off in a subdued frame of mind.'

'I can take care of myself too,' Abigail protested as he took her arm and led her to the taxi that waited by the steps. He never missed an opportunity to remind her that he thought her incompetent, she thought.

'We'll not be putting that to the test, though,' he murmured sardonically, glancing down at her beautiful face and her slender shape in the lovely gown. 'Wild declarations have never influenced me. You stepped out of the bright cloud of morning, a flower fairy. Fenella could hold her own in a black hole and defeat the magnetic force. If he tries any of his tricks with her, he'll be savaged.'

Probably, Abigail thought grimly. No doubt the two of them would make a very stunning couple but she knew who Fenella would attach herself to the moment they arrived at this club. Logan settled her in the taxi and then ignored her for the whole of the journey. Luckily it was not far, because his deep silence and his expression only added to her nervous tension.

Whatever emotions he felt, he was holding them in tight check. When he had taken her arm his fingers had sent an electric current of desire to her own skin. He was furious with himself for wanting her, his anger keeping him silent, and she knew that if she had possessed any sense at all she would have been feeling triumphant at this victory.

She felt nothing of the sort, though, because in spite of her breathless awareness of his feelings she knew that they did not spring from love. Love was kind, gentle; it forgave. Logan would never forgive and one day his desire would fade. Perhaps if she had stayed with him it would have faded already.

*   *   *

The club was glittering with lights, music swirling out into the warm night air. It was a place for the very rich and that was only too obvious. Once again it was set in gardens; the high gates they had passed through were guarded and closed behind them with the smooth movement of well-oiled mechanisms. Through the lighted windows, Abigail could see the glitter of chandeliers and the brilliant colours of many expensive gowns. She was greatly relieved to know that her own gown would not be at all out of place in this atmosphere, more greatly relieved still when she saw Fenella.

They were standing waiting for them—Grant and his wife, Pete Cassidy and Fenella—and as Logan paid off the taxi Grant came down the steps to greet her.

'You make me glad to be still alive,' he told her as he took her arm gently. 'I'm not even sure I can stand it.'

Abigail laughed, looking up to see Ivy Cassidy beaming at her, and she carefully avoided looking at the other two. Ivy's hair was blonde tonight and Grant noticed Abigail's stare of astonishment.

'A wig, a wig,' he muttered soothingly, patting her hand as it lay against his arm. 'It's her hobby. She's done this sort of thing all her life. I think it's supposed to keep me interested. Mostly it brings me close to a fainting spell.'

He was laughing and Ivy heard most of it. She grinned at Abigail, as irrepressible as her husband.

'Well, I decided I just couldn't compete with that hair,' she explained, nodding in the direction of Abigail's shining head. 'I'll go off black, I think. It's too easy to tell when it's fake.'

'Isn't it, though?' Pete Cassidy murmured, coming to force himself close to Abigail. 'I can't believe what I'm

seeing. When I met you the other day I was stunned.
Now I'm not even sure if you're real.'

'She's only real for me,' Logan assured him tightly,
coming up and taking Abigail's wrist in a possessive grip.
'To anyone else she's merely an illusion.'

The Cassidys were talking to Fenella by now and
missed this little exchange and their absence seemed to
make Pete Cassidy more bold. He lost his coolly insolent expression.

'In other words, hands off,' he said grimly, glaring at
Logan.

'In *plain* words,' Logan corrected him menacingly,
'this is my wife.'

'Sure,' Pete Cassidy replied, his usual expression back
in place at Logan's tone. 'Did I doubt it? Compli-
menting a beautiful woman comes naturally to me, I
guess. They usually like it.'

'Perhaps their husbands don't,' Logan suggested
acidly. 'I seem to think that Miss Mitchell is your partner
this evening.'

Pete Cassidy looked across at Fenella with a wry grin.

'That lady is tough,' he commented, and Logan led
Abigail away, his hand firm and warm against her back.

'I thought you'd notice,' he murmured drily.

Fenella had noticed too. She was too far away to have
heard this icy little clash but her eyes were taking in each
expression, from Abigail's flushed embarrassment and
Pete Cassidy's speculative glances to Logan's grim annoyance. She came drifting forward and attached herself
to Logan, clinging to his arm.

'I thought you'd never get here,' she said in a low,
sultry voice. 'What odd people. Let's get this deal over
with and get back to London.'

Abigail stiffened; she couldn't help it even though she knew that Logan felt her reaction. Oh, yes, Fenella would be anxious to get back to London. She wondered if that sultry voice was ever used in the boardroom or if she reserved it merely for Logan.

After that, Grant took over and the evening became more relaxed. The club was huge, rivalling anything that London could offer, and even Fenella seemed impressed. Abigail looked at her secretly. She had never had a good look at this woman before and she had to admit that Fenella Mitchell was beautiful.

Her hair was smoothly straight, with none of the swirling curls that had been Abigail's problem all her life. The smooth, honey-blonde hair gave Fenella that air of sophistication that Abigail felt she never seemed to achieve. Her clothes were beautiful too—her dress a sheath of dark blue silk that clung to a slim figure. She didn't look like a lawyer, Abigail concluded. She could have been a model or an actress. It was only her eyes that gave her away. They were an icy blue, watchful, intelligent and hard.

They were hard as they glanced at Abigail and the smile she sent in Abigail's direction was frosty and knowing. Fenella hadn't lost as far as Logan was concerned; her expression said as much and she wanted Abigail to know it.

After dinner the party went on. There was dancing but Abigail found herself captured by Grant and Ivy. They seemed to be delighted with her and took her off to meet other people. It made her more at ease but she was painfully aware all the time that this was playing right into Fenella's hands. Each time she looked round, Logan seemed to be in deep conversation with Fenella, and he only moved away from her when Pete Cassidy came back from greeting friends and took up his obvious duty as escort to Logan's lawyer.

She couldn't escape dancing with Logan but he hardly spoke and all the time Abigail's eyes strayed to the other woman. She was quite surprised to find that Fenella seemed to be enjoying her talk with Pete Cassidy. Each time she noticed them they were deep in conversation and her heart skipped a beat when from time to time they looked across at her.

She told herself that Fenella would, in fact, be watching Logan but even so she knew it wasn't true. The coldly blue eyes fastened on her with too much attention for her to be mistaken. There was something going on there that she could not fathom and it worried her. If Fenella Mitchell was talking to Pete Cassidy in any pleasant way then it was to gain some advantage for herself.

After a while she found herself back with Grant and Ivy, and Logan danced with Fenella. She tried not to notice how the other woman's hand moved possessively on Logan's sleeve but she couldn't stop looking and she was quite unprepared when Pete Cassidy appeared and demanded a dance.

He didn't ask. His tone was not at all quietly persuasive but, with his parents there, Abigail felt unable to refuse. She steeled herself for the ordeal and managed a brittle smile that quite clearly amused him in the worst possible manner.

'So,' he probed as soon as they had danced away from the others, 'you and Logan are separated.'

'Of course we're not separated,' Abigail managed quickly. 'Does it look like it?'

Now she knew what Fenella had been whispering to this odious creature. Could it be that Miss Mitchell did not know the whole story about Grant's insistence on a happily married man to buy his business? She was utterly in the dark, thrown in alone without Logan to help and she could only play it by ear.

'It doesn't look like it,' he agreed sarcastically. 'It looks just too good to be true in fact. I've never met such a jealous husband before.'

'Well, I'm sure you must be an expert on husbands,' Abigail murmured with a sarcasm of her own. 'In this case, however, you've been misinformed.'

'I don't think so, babe,' he sneered. 'Separate rooms means separated and, according to my information, you've got the best rooms in the hotel, next door to each other.'

'How dare you speak to me like this?' Abigail stormed, more angry than worried by now. 'Our affairs do not even remotely concern you.'

'They would concern my father,' he murmured slyly, dancing her into a corner away from prying eyes. 'I could be persuaded not to tell him, though.'

Abigail pulled violently to get free but he merely laughed and tightened his hold on her and she was struggling so much that neither of them saw Logan. The first thing that Abigail knew was that Pete Cassidy's face went into a spasm of pain as Logan's hand gripped his neck from behind like a vice.

'Didn't I tell you to keep away from my wife?' Logan asked through clenched teeth. 'I can see that words alone do not impress you.'

His hand moved to Pete Cassidy's shoulder and Abigail watched with wide, shocked eyes as Logan's grip hardened and the other man began to sink slowly to his knees.

It was impossible that this should go unnoticed and Abigail tried to stop it.

'Logan! Please!' she said urgently. She had never seen him like this before. His anger made her tremble and she was almost relieved when Grant appeared, his face a picture of astonishment and annoyance.

'What the hell is this?' he wanted to know, and his voice seemed to penetrate to Logan. He relaxed his hold and Grant saw his son stagger and slowly stand upright, his hand clasping his shoulder. His face was completely white and he just pushed past everyone and walked out of the club.

Logan reached for Abigail and pulled her to him before turning blazing eyes on Grant.

'When I see somebody manhandling my wife, I see red at the same time,' he said coldly. 'What it was about, I'll find out; meanwhile, we're leaving. If this deal is on, Grant, we sign tomorrow morning, otherwise forget it. We're going home tomorrow with or without the deal.'

Ivy came up and went to Abigail at once, her eyes on the slender arms that were already bruising.

'Oh, honey, look!' she said to Grant in a shocked whisper, and the anger died from Grant's face at this proof.

'I'll take this up with him at home,' he promised. 'Don't worry about the deal, Logan. That young man has a lot of explaining to do.'

Logan was in no mood to be placated and he began to take Abigail away, his arm tightly around her shoulders.

'I'm not worrying about the deal,' he ground out, not one bit mollified. 'I can take it or leave it. Let me know tomorrow—early.'

Abigail found herself being led to the door and by now almost every eye in the club was on them.

'Don't let it embarrass you,' Logan muttered, his face still filled with fury, and she felt like laughing hysterically.

'I'm not embarrassed,' she whispered, fighting to keep a grip on her swaying emotions. 'I'm just wondering what that little creep will tell Grant when he gets home. He announced that he knew we were separated.'

'Did he?' Logan muttered, as if he was only vaguely interested.

'You're not taking this seriously enough,' she pointed out, almost trotting to keep up with him. 'When Grant finds out, the deal will be off.'

Logan swore under his breath but it was more a comment on his own annoyed feelings than any concern about the deal and Abigail sighed as she sank, still shaking, into a taxi with Logan beside her.

The whole thing had come apart. All this trauma, all this distress had been for nothing. She had been forced close to Logan again, forced to acknowledge her love all over again and the whole thing had been useless. She couldn't tell him what she suspected—that Fenella had lured Pete Cassidy into that nasty little scene—and when they got back to the hotel he would want to know everything that had happened.

She rested back against the seat, tired and utterly depressed. Whatever she thought, she had to keep it to herself because Logan would suspect that she was simply jealous and trying to get Fenella into trouble.

He took her straight to her room, closed the door and turned on her, nothing about his expression leading her to believe that he would be put off by excuses.

'Word for word!' he ordered sharply, fixing her with that grey-eyed stare.

'There were few words. He asked me to dance—no, he *told* me to dance and then he came straight out with it. He announced that you and I are separated. He even knew about the separate rooms.'

'Why didn't you just walk off?' Logan grated, and she turned annoyed eyes on him.

'You saw the results of my attempt at that. I could have hit him, of course, but I decided to leave the big scene for you.'

'What did you expect me to do—laugh it off?' Logan snarled, and Abigail sighed and turned away.

'No. I was glad to see you but this makes it awkward. When he faces Grant tonight he's going to tell everything he knows or thinks he knows and that's the end of this deal.'

'Damn the deal!' Logan muttered. He went to the phone and spoke sharply. 'A tray of tea for my wife,' he ordered. 'Make it fast.'

When he turned round, some of the temper had died on his face but he looked suspiciously thoughtful.

'Get into your dressing gown,' he suggested moodily. 'You'll be more comfortable.'

It sounded like a good idea and there was always the chance that when she came out of the bathroom he would be gone. For one thing, he had abandoned Fenella at the club, and even though that lady was capable of fighting off a hoard of barbarians leaving a guest alone was not quite Logan's style.

She disappeared into the bathroom and took off the lovely dress, quite glum that she had not been able to wear it in better circumstances. She lingered, cleaning her face and brushing her hair out, but when she came back Logan was still there. He had flung himself into a

chair and she could tell by the signs on that clever face
that he was doing some fast thinking.

He pointed to the tray of tea that had already been
delivered and as she poured a cup he watched her steadily
before saying, 'So Fenella tried to sink the ship. Why
not come right out and say it?'

'I'm not competent to speculate on big business deals,'
Abigail murmured carefully. 'In any case, he simply said
it was according to his information. Maybe it was a
waiter. One of them is a gossip.'

'Nice try, Abigail,' Logan drawled sardonically. 'To
the best of my knowledge, Snake Eyes hasn't been in
this place since we came except to collect Fenella tonight. At that time, he didn't wander far from my icy
glance. Nobody spoke to him. I was hard pressed to
speak to him myself.'

Abigail's lips twitched in amusement at Logan's name
for Pete Cassidy. That was exactly how she thought of
him herself; all the same, she wasn't going to be drawn
into any speculation about Fenella Mitchell.

'Well, I can't see what she could possibly have to gain,'
she murmured, 'and she has plenty to lose.'

'Knowing how your mind works, I won't ask what,'
he replied ironically. 'Drink your tea. I'll get to the
bottom of this tomorrow.'

'I don't expect there'll be any deal now,' Abigail
sighed. 'He's sure to tell Grant what he thinks even if
only to get himself out of trouble. Add that to the considerable pain he suffered and it seems to be the end of
any kind of business.'

'You think I should have walked up and pretended
not to notice?' Logan asked drily. And she shook her
head vigorously, a shudder running over her skin at the
memory of that unpleasant interlude. 'As to the deal,'

he continued, 'it's not all that important. I've already got a stake in this country that makes Grant's business look insignificant.'

'Then why...?' Abigail stared at him in astonishment and he stood, slanting her an amused sideways glance as he walked to the door.

'The machinations of a devious mind.' He stopped and turned, coming back towards her. 'Let me look at those arms. He mauled you considerably.'

Before she could stop him he had pushed up the sleeves of her dressing gown and was studying the growing bruises with angry, narrowed eyes.

'I should have squeezed his neck a damned sight harder,' he muttered. 'Does it hurt?'

He looked up at her with a slight anxiety on his face and she shook her head. For once, he looked almost vulnerable, and a small smile crept unbidden to her face.

'Not much. I'll bathe my arms in cold water.'

'Shall I ring down and get you something for it? There are all-night chemists here.'

'It's all right, Logan, really,' Abigail assured him. Unthinkingly she put her hand on his arm, and he looked down at her slender fingers, so pale against his dark sleeve. When he looked up, his expression had warmed and he took her face between his hands, kissing her lips carefully and softly.

'All right, sweet Abbie. If you need me, I'm just next door.'

'Aren't you going back for Fenella?' she asked, and she got that tilted grin again.

'I think not. If she gets very uptight about being deserted, she's probably innocent of the charges. If she lets the matter drop, then she's most probably guilty.'

'You don't know that,' Abigail reminded him swiftly, and he gave her another quick glance as he left.

'I don't *know* it,' he agreed quietly. 'It's a matter of instinct and your instincts were always better than mine. What do you think, Abbie?'

'How could I know?' she said quickly, and Logan looked at her steadily.

'You watched her all evening. Mischief usually brews up quite visibly.' He went out, leaving Abigail wondering where this left her and exactly where this left Logan. Why didn't he care about this deal when he had dragged her over here to clinch the matter? Now he seemed to be utterly unconcerned, as if he was the one doing Grant a favour.

She gave herself a little mental shake. It was impossible to follow Logan's way of thinking but clearly, somewhere along the line, she had missed an important fact. She surely hoped that they were going tomorrow and that she would not have to see the hideous Pete Cassidy again.

She went to bathe her arms and really they were hurting quite a lot. There were fingermarks that were deepening by the minute and any sight of them in the morning would merely infuriate Logan again.

Abigail was up quite early the next day and there was no sign of Logan. Somehow, last night had left her feeling more sure of herself because he had certainly been protective. There had been no pretence about his fury and it had not all been jealousy alone. She decided to eat downstairs. She was not going to skulk in her room like a frightened child. If Fenella was there she might just give herself away and admit to telling Pete Cassidy about the separation.

There was no sign of Logan or Fenella, though, and Abigail couldn't help the little sinking of her heart when she found that they were both out. Again her informant was the waiter and she gave him a very brittle smile for this information. Why couldn't people mind their own business? Some things she just didn't want to know.

'They ate earlier,' he said, and she dismissed him with a curt nod of her head.

Afterwards she went for what would very likely be her last walk on the beach—because she knew Logan. He would not stay here now, even if the affair was concluded amicably. It was a shame that this lovely place had been merely the setting for an act of deceit—an act she had been forced into. It would have been nice to be here for a holiday. But only with Logan, her mind assured her. She was not interested in being here either alone or with anyone else.

He was there when she came back, watching her from the balcony again, but this time he did not remonstrate with her at all.

'We're leaving this morning,' he told her when she came into her room.

'I'll be ready.' It was all she was prepared to say because she didn't want to know what had happened; at least, she didn't want to know that this subterfuge and her own misery had all been for nothing.

'We can stay and have a real holiday if you like,' Logan said quietly as he watched her downcast face, and her head shot up, her eyes green and wide.

'A holiday? Oh, Logan, don't offer a continuation of a nightmare as if you're wanting to do me a favour. I can't get out of here fast enough. And, whatever happens, I've done my part. Don't forget that. It was not my fault that we ran into a lunatic.'

Logan's brow darkened at her tone but he nodded seriously, keeping his temper.

'No. It was not your fault at all. You played the part very well, Abigail. You even acted above and beyond the call of duty.'

There was no mistaking what he meant and Abigail's face flushed as he stared at her icily.

'So you'll help out the Madden Corporation?' she insisted, and he turned away, shrugging dismissively.

'I've already said so. I gave you my word. The fiasco last night was not your fault. In any case, it made little or no difference, although there is now a certain strain between Grant and myself. I signed the deal this morning.'

'With Fenella?' She couldn't stop the words coming out and he turned and looked at her bleakly.

'Naturally with Fenella. I told you she had to countersign.'

'So she's flying back with us?' Abigail said quietly, and he muttered under his breath as he stalked towards the door.

'She's already left. I had a job for her in New York. You and I are going home.'

'She won't like being left behind,' Abigail persisted foolishly, and he turned a grey-eyed stare of annoyance on her.

'What she likes or does not like is of no importance. She works for me and she has a damned good job. If she wants to keep it, she does exactly as she is told and goes exactly where I send her. Pack your clothes, Abigail, and don't fight out of your league, especially as you're not prepared to play your ace card at any time.'

'I don't have an ace,' Abigail pointed out miserably, and he turned in the doorway at the last minute, his eyes on her face.

'Oh, yes, you do, Abigail,' he insisted softly. 'The trouble is, you've never recognised it.'

CHAPTER NINE

AFTER the glorious sunshine of California, London was grey and dismal. There had been a heavy downpour just before the plane landed. Abigail looked out of the taxi window as they sped along in the gathering dusk. Beside her, Logan was silent, tensed up and she sat in equal silence, almost holding her breath, afraid to say even one word in case it was the wrong one.

They had not made any sort of plan but it was obviously necessary to go to the flat first. Logan had collected her and returned to the flat before their trip to America and his car was there. Abigail's car was at home.

She almost grimaced just thinking the word and the old line 'Home is where the heart is' ran unbidden through her mind. Her heart was and always would be with Logan. From now on she would not be content to stay with her father and she knew it. She was not even willing to stay with the Madden Corporation when he was fit to return to his office.

The viability or not of her father's firm depended solely on Logan and, whether it succeeded or not, she would move now and take another job. She ran the thought through her mind, her hopes resting on Brian Wingate. He was unlikely to refuse to employ her with his firm, even though Logan had told him clearly to keep away from her. Even so, going straight to Brian and starting there seemed an easy option. Easy for her but not for Brian. There was no knowing how Logan would take it.

'Come into the flat.'

Abigail came back to the present to find the taxi halted outside the flat and Logan preparing to pay the driver. He was dealing with their luggage and at the sound of Logan's dark voice Abigail felt a sharp attack of nerves threatening.

'Is it necessary?' she asked in a low voice, turning away from the taxi driver's alert ears. 'Can't you just take me straight home?'

'I want to talk to you,' Logan insisted, aiming one of his coolly dismissive stares at the driver, who hastened away. He picked up most of their luggage, leaving just two small bags for Abigail. 'A drink and a few words and I'll have you on your way.'

She nodded as calmly as possible. Was this where he told her that she could now go about getting that divorce? Was he going to lay down new rules about his aid to the firm? Whatever it was, he seemed to be determined, and she had no means of getting back home without his aid.

With the lights on in the flat the gathering gloom of the outside was dispelled but another gloom descended on Abigail. This was probably the last time she would ever be here in this place where she had been so heavenly happy and then so terribly unhappy. It was too poignant for her to take any last look around and she stood in the centre of the sitting room, her hands clasped loosely in front of her.

Logan glanced at her sceptically and then poured a drink, offering her one.

'I'd rather have tea,' she managed evenly, and he shrugged, sitting down and looking up at her quizzically.

'You know where the kitchen is. It's your kitchen.'

It was deliberately provocative and Abigail decided to ignore it. She went through to the kitchen and busied herself with making tea, her ears attuned to any move he might make. It was nerve-racking to wait for his announcement, whatever it was. There was always something simmering in Logan's brilliant mind. Every move was thought out with meticulous care.

When she went back in, he was stretched out in the chair, his head resting back, his eyes closed, and Abigail sat down carefully, quite prepared to wait and definitely not willing to prompt him. He looked tired, as if he were carrying some great burden, and she wondered if he thought now of his mother and father. Did the memory of them eat into his days? Was that why over the last four years he had become almost superhuman to most people in the business world with his astonishing ability to work all hours?

His lashes shadowed his high cheekbones, faint lines of weariness showed around his eyes and she longed for the right to go across and kneel in front of him, to rest her head against his knee in the way she had done so often when they'd been together.

'What are your plans?'

The grey eyes had opened. He was watching her and Abigail gave a guilty start before she answered.

'That all depends on how you intend to act,' she said quietly. 'If you're coming in to take over then I'll have to be there to brief you, I suppose. After that, I intend to leave. If, on the other hand, you're going to work from the background and help that way then I'll have to stay until my father is able to take over. That being the case, I'll leave then.'

'And go where?' he asked shortly.

'Wingate's. I was offered a job there a long time ago. That's what Brian was talking to me about when . . .'

'When I savaged him,' Logan finished for her irascibly. He sat up and pinned her with cold eyes. 'You've worked damned hard these past few years and one day that firm will be yours. What's the point of getting out now when it could all be salvaged and working well within months?'

'Self-preservation,' Abigail answered calmly. 'I want a new life, another life. I intend to start again before I get enmeshed in anything at all.' She made a decision to bring matters to a head now rather than wait in misery. 'I'll apply for a divorce as you suggested. That can be seen to at once, no matter what is happening in the firm.'

Logan leaned back again and regarded her blandly.

'I'll oppose any divorce,' he informed her with no inflection at all in his voice.

It stunned her into silence for a second and Abigail looked at him in astonishment.

'You said... The night you were so nasty to Brian, you said I should go ahead and get a divorce.'

'From time to time I lose my temper,' Logan reminded her silkily. 'I'm not in a rage now and, I repeat, I will oppose any divorce.'

'You can't. We've been separated for a long time. Even if you're serious about this I can get a divorce next year with or without your consent. It would be a mere formality.'

'I'm serious,' Logan assured her. 'And next year would not make five years' continuous separation. We've been lovers twice in the last week. We're reconciled in the eyes of the world. No divorce, Abigail.'

She remembered his words in the flat, at the hotel— words of desire—and now every sense came to danger alert. The lovemaking had been part of some plan and once again, as always with Logan, she had fallen for it.

'It was all deliberate,' she whispered. 'You even planned . . . planned—that.'

'You helped.' His lips twisted wryly. 'I don't remember you putting up any sort of struggle, Abigail. All I remember is that you went off into space just as you've always done. If I had a plan then you were a very willing accomplice.' He stared at her with narrowed eyes, glittering and grey. 'It was no great hardship to want you—I always have done, from the moment I first saw you.'

'Take me home!' She stood and glared at him because it was the only thing she could safely do. There was no clue as to the state of his mind in his expression. For reasons she could not fathom he was opposing any divorce and although she could simply go ahead, call his bluff she knew his ways. He did not mean that he would oppose things in any calm and easy way. Logan always had some plan.

'You can stay here,' he suggested, his eyes never leaving her. 'It's better than that great, cold house you've occupied for the past four years. To the whole world, we're reconciled. Let them go on thinking that. I have no doubt at all that under the new circumstances your father would be delighted.'

'What new circumstances?' She still stood waiting although Logan hadn't moved to obey when she had demanded to go home.

'Don't be obtuse, Abigail,' he murmured, getting to his feet slowly. 'I'm supposed to be helping. Sooner or later, Kent Madden will have to work with me. He'll seem less like a man who is taking charity if his saviour is his son-in-law, happily reunited with his only daughter.'

Abigail found her mind working overtime but even so she could not see beyond the moment. That Logan was

planning some further mischief was evident but what
that mischief would be she had no way of knowing. The
old fear came racing back.

'You made a promise,' she choked. 'I pretended to be
reconciled. I kept my half of the bargain. You said you
would pull the Madden Corporation together. You gave
your word.'

'I'll keep it,' he assured her softly. 'The trouble is,
Abigail, that having had you back for a while, I want
you back permanently. Come back to me and your father
is right off the hook.'

'You promised!' She stared at him with wide, frustrated eyes and he shrugged easily, a slight smile hov-
ering over his lips.

'I promised to help the firm. I said nothing at all about
letting your father step free. I've never felt inclined to
do that. There are more ways than one of seeking
revenge.'

'What are you going to do?'

Abigail was mesmerised by the clever, handsome face
and his slight smile grew into a wide and amused one as
he looked back at her.

'I see you have that expression on your face again,'
he murmured ironically. 'Once again you're certain of
my omnipotence. As to what I intend to do, I never show
my hand until the circumstances are right. I've waited
a long time. I can wait further—if you're prepared to
risk it.'

She felt a wave of anger then. Trapped! Always she
had been trapped, first by her love for Logan and then
by her loyalty to her father. Now Logan was coolly inviting her into a new trap and she had no doubt at all
that he would use her as he had always used her—to gain
his own ends. He had not asked her to go back to him

because he loved her. He did not love her and never had done. It was merely a dark threat—his way of playing on her conscience and her loyalty.

'Nice try but hard luck,' she said scornfully, taking great pleasure in looking at him disdainfully. 'You're counting on my loyalty to my father. You're counting on my well-known guilty conscience. But this time, Logan, you've guessed wrongly. I don't feel the same any more. Once, I would have done anything you asked, just because I was bewitched. I'm no longer bewitched.'

The smile had died on his face and now he looked at her bleakly. Abigail felt a wave of triumph. Once, just once, she would fool Logan. If she could get out of here without showing that her love for him was greater than ever then she would have won.

'As to my father,' she continued when he said nothing at all, 'I don't trust him any more than I trust you. These past few weeks have shown me that there's not really a lot to choose between you. You're both prepared to use me to gain your own ends. Well, this time I'm not falling for anything. We'll simply stick to the bargain as laid down and I'll hold you to your word. After that, I'll leave and set up a new life that will not contain either of you. I told you I was tired of being pig-in-the-middle. I meant it. Brian Wingate wants me in his firm and it's not for any male chauvinist reason. I'm good at what I do, Logan. I intend to go out into the world and do it.'

'You want to hear me say I love you?' he asked quietly, and she turned away, picking up her bag and small case.

'Don't bother to lie,' she said flatly. 'You never have lied and it's a little late to start now. In any case, I no longer care. I simply want to go home. My part of the deal is over.'

Abigail walked purposefully to the door and although her legs were shaking she knew she had fooled him. He said nothing more. He simply picked up her cases and followed, and it was all over.

Logan didn't appear at the offices of the Madden Corporation. From the time that Abigail returned on the following Monday, it was obvious that new life was being pumped into the place but it was being done from a distance; Logan was not about to enter the place he hated. There was almost the old bustle about the offices and although it was a relief to find that Logan was in action, pulling strings from far away, Abigail also felt sadness. The busy offices, the new life about the place served to remind her of how things had been on the day she had met Logan here for the first time.

He'd sent in one of his top men, a man called Joe Saville—a middle-aged genius who worked with Abigail and delved deeply into the business of the firm. He could scarcely be called a fatherly man but gradually she relaxed with him and became quite enthusiastic. She was learning a lot and his sharp, pleased glances in her direction when she offered any suggestion made her feel that Brian had not been merely kind when he had told her she was good.

Her father progressed, his attitude one that went well on its way to infuriating her. Now that the firm was out of danger he was striking an attitude and although he had not as yet set foot in the place he interfered with almost everything she planned, treating her, as usual, as if she were an imbecile.

Fortunately, Joe Saville merely grunted at the messages she brought and went about his business in his own way. He had to report to Logan every evening, he told her, and this was more a worry to him than any mere chance of upsetting Kent Madden.

Abigail could only agree. There was also a strange kind of comfort in knowing that Logan went over everything and her cheeks flushed when she wondered if Joe Saville told him about the things she had suggested herself. She threw herself enthusiastically into the work because she could not afford to allow herself the time to think about Logan. She had always missed him but now, after their trip together, she found each lonely night an added misery. She loved him, she wanted his arms around her, but not without love.

One night the following week she left work early and went to do some shopping. The days, though still warm, were shorter and by the time Abigail had finished her shopping the shop windows were bright with lights and the sky was deepening to evening.

'Why, it's Logan's wife!' Abigail turned from her last-minute window-shopping to find herself confronted and almost trapped by Fenella Mitchell. 'I hear the Madden Corporation is thriving again,' she continued before Abigail could escape. 'The city is quite enthralled, holding its breath, so to speak. Of course, now that you're back with Logan it's all explained.'

'Is it?' Abigail murmured. 'The city keeps an eye on Logan's private life then, does it?'

'Well, he's not just any man, is he?' Fenella asked with a knowing smile. 'There has always been this sort of morbid interest, ever since his father committed suicide, but even without that he's such a brilliant man. Naturally the city takes an interest.'

Abigail stood as if she had been carved from stone, the words ringing in her head. People bumped into her

and she didn't even react. All she could hear were the
words 'ever since his father committed suicide' and she
simply stared at Fenella, aware of nothing else.

'What do you mean?' she asked in a strange voice,
and Fenella raised dark, shapely brows.

'But didn't you know? You must have done. Everyone
knows. That's what brought Logan back to England
from America; that's why he stayed here instead of going
back. He owns far more there than he does here. And
I should know,' she added with a frown. 'I'm usually
dispatched to see to things. I fly out there with Joe
Saville, although I hear he's now working with you.'

Abigail still stood silently; another person bumped into
her and Fenella took her arm impatiently.

'You're going to be knocked over soon. I had no idea
that my little bit of gossip would stun you. I imagined
that Logan would have told you. Come and have a
coffee. You'd better sit down at the very least.'

Abigail knew dimly that she was playing right into
Fenella's hands but at that moment she felt incapable
of defending herself. If it were true, if Logan's father
had indeed taken his own life, then that was the cause
of Logan's deadly vendetta and it would never end.

'There. You look quite shocked.' Fenella settled them
at a table and flung up her hand imperiously for the
waiter. 'I would never have told you but, after all, you
were Logan's wife!'

'I still am Logan's wife,' Abigail said quietly, striving
to defend herself, however feebly. She had no illusions.
This had been quite deliberate. How it would serve
Fenella's purpose she didn't know but she could not now
simply let the matter rest. For five years she had been
trying to find out how her father had made such an

enemy of Logan and now she was about to learn everything.

'Why?' she asked quietly. 'What made Logan's father...?'

'He was tricked, cheated and ruined,' Fenella assured her. She sipped her coffee with every appearance of enjoyment and Abigail had no doubt at all that she was also enjoying this conversation. 'He was a property dealer,' Fenella continued. 'He was well liked and completely honest. Like Logan, his word was his bond, accepted throughout the city. There was a lot of competition, of course, but he built up the Steele Group slowly and surely, completely above board.'

She looked at Abigail's pale face and seemed determined to make her beg for information and Abigail had no choice.

'So what went wrong?' she asked.

'Jealousy and greed,' Fenella stated. 'Some people are not content to work and wait. Some people want it all and they want it now, even things that don't belong to them.' She fixed Abigail with pitying eyes. 'Surely you know that your father drove John Steele to suicide? How can you not have known? It was all over the papers, although no mention was made of names and nothing could ever be proved. It was well-known that your father used various agents to dupe John Steele into buying land that was never going to get planning consent. The whole city lives on borrowing and the land deal was enormous. The whole thing crashed like a pack of cards and your father went for the jugular, trying to buy out the Steele Group for next to nothing. It wasn't even that, though, that drove John Steele to his death. He had borrowed money he could never pay back, made promises he could never keep, and he couldn't live with it. He stood to lose everything, even his home. He drove his car off the Embankment.'

'Perhaps—perhaps it was an accident.' Abigail whispered. She had no heart even to try to defend her father, not even to this woman whose cold blue eyes enjoyed everything.

'That was the verdict,' Fenella said scathingly, 'but everyone knew differently. The insurance money would have kept his wife safe at least.'

'She died,' Abigail managed to get out unevenly.

'She was very ill already,' Fenella informed her. 'It was something they had kept to themselves. Losing John was too much for her. She died in the same week. Logan never even got to see them again.'

'Logan was rich,' Abigail protested. 'He would have helped.'

'He wasn't rich then. His wealth came soon after and it took real wealth to save the Steele Group.'

'But his grandfather, his uncle—why didn't Logan's father appeal to them?'

'I suppose you've never heard of pride, honour?' Fenella asked scornfully, getting her things together, ready to leave. 'After all, your father hasn't had much of the latter and you have little pride, going back to Logan after all this time. You know he still sees me; you knew when you were married. I can only assume you've gone back to him so that he'll save your father after spending years destroying him. But don't hold your breath. Logan still wants revenge and, knowing him, he'll get it one way or the other.'

'I know that,' Abigail said, getting to her feet. 'For your information, I have not gone back to Logan. I'm working to get the Madden Corporation back on its feet and then I'll be right out of your lives. You can see each other whenever you wish.'

'We do!' Fenella swept out of the restaurant and Abigail gathered her bag and left the money for the coffee on the table. Her legs felt as if they would not hold her up and she had cold knowledge inside her. Now she knew why Logan hated so much, why her father feared him, because although she had no reason to trust Fenella Mitchell in anything her heart told her that this was only the truth. And Logan's words at his office came back to her. 'Promises to keep, Abigail.'

Logan's life was built on promises and his father's life had been built on them too. John Steele had not been able to keep his promises and the dishonour had served to kill him. Logan would keep his promise. This would never end.

She didn't go in to see her father in the hospital. She couldn't face him. She only had a vague idea of what had really happened. Only Logan could tell her the complete truth and Abigail had the terrible feeling that her father would not even offer excuses. He would say it was business practice. Perhaps it was but it was discreditable, corrupt, and while at one time she would have staunchly defended him, said it could not possibly be true, she could not do that now because in her heart she knew it was near enough to the truth.

Now it seemed almost like a rough sort of justice that Logan had begun his campaign by taking her away from her father. It had been his first line of attack, his first action and since then he had been steadily wiping the Madden Corporation out. He had outbid them in every project, used his wealth to squeeze them out of business and had still, with his brilliance, made a profit for his company when profits should have been almost nonexistent. He was helping now because he had some terrible plan—something much worse than anything he had done before.

Next day she was tired and quiet at the office and Joe Saville looked at her out of the corner of his eye, asking nothing but clearly thinking a great deal. By lunchtime she could not contain her emotions any longer and as the small dining room was almost empty she tried to find out more, tried to wipe out Fenella's cold words.

'How long have you been with Logan?' she asked him when they were sitting at a table and everyone else had left.

'Almost six years. I joined him soon after he came back from the States. The Steele Group was practically on its knees at the time. Logan just threw money and expertise into it and worked as I've never seen a man work before. I don't know, but I heard that the banks were a little scared to back him at first. Apparently he stormed in and more or less threw money at them. He's got enormous holdings in the States.' He suddenly looked red-faced. 'I don't know why I'm telling you all this. You're his wife. You probably know a lot more than I do.'

'I don't know a lot about his father,' Abigail ventured carefully. 'I only found out yesterday that—that there was a suspicion that he had taken his own life.'

Joe Saville frowned and glanced at her uneasily.

'A bad business, that. There were rumours flying around even when I joined the Steele Group but you know how it is—these things are only news for a while. As far as I know, nothing came out officially.'

No, it wouldn't, Abigail mused bleakly. Logan had said that the law would never catch her father but he had caught him. The fact that he appeared to have let him go made no sense at all, unless he had something worse planned. And it could only be for that reason that he had asked her to go back to him. He wanted her father isolated when the final blow came. He wanted him to be alone and unaided as his own father had been.

She went to the small, luxurious hospital that night. Her father was now almost ready to come home—they had told her that the previous week—and she had to tackle him before then. If what Fenella had told her was true then she just would not be there when he came out. He could live as he liked to live and take her place at the office.

He was looking well and smiled broadly when he saw her, ignoring the fact that she had not visited the previous night.

'You look tired, Abigail,' he observed. 'Is that husband of yours running you off your feet at the office? He's a hard taskmaster, according to the rumours.'

'He's never been in,' she said steadily. 'I work with Joe Saville and he reports to Logan. Things are picking up rapidly. In fact, I can't see how Logan's managing it so quickly.'

'Probably channelling back some of the business he stole from us in the first place,' her father muttered irascibly. 'I can't think why he's doing this anyway. He hasn't a weak spot in his whole armour; if he had had, I would have found it.'

'No, he's not weak,' Abigail agreed. 'Maybe he learned not to be, after his father died.'

'What do you mean?' Kent Madden sat up in his chair and glared at her. 'His father wasn't just weak, he was a fool.'

'An honourable fool?' Abigail asked quietly. 'Is that how you managed to trick him?'

'I don't know what Steele's been telling you—' her father began, and she interrupted coldly, her eyes never leaving his face.

'I haven't seen Logan at all. I had my information from another source entirely. Logan would never tell me anything about this vendetta; neither would you. Is it because you caused his father's death?'

'I didn't drive his car into the river,' he snapped, his face reddening with anger. 'He was stupid enough to take everything on trust and he lost his firm. What he did after that was his own idea.'

'After you'd left him with nothing, not even his dignity and honour,' Abigail accused him, and he leaned back, laughing that cold laugh she had heard before so many times in her life.

'You can't bank dignity and honour,' he assured her sarcastically. 'You listen to any lame-dog story. Business is cutthroat; it's either sink or swim. John Steele just took everything on trust—a fool. You're a fool too, Abigail. Too soft to succeed. You always were.'

'Not now,' she said, getting to her feet and preparing to leave. 'I always blamed Logan for not loving me when I loved him so much. How could he have loved me? How could I have expected it? His whole life was poisoned and you did it. I'm not a fool any more. I learn quite quickly when I know the truth and I know it now.'

'So what are you going to do?' he asked scathingly. 'Run back to Logan Steele?'

'How can I?' she asked, looking at him as if she had never seen him before. 'I'm the one doing the loving, not Logan. No, I'm not running back to him. I'm just leaving altogether. When you want to go back to the office, it's still there. And it's all your problem.'

'Come back here!' he grated angrily, but Abigail just walked out. She had taken all she was about to take and there was nowhere she wanted to be but with Logan. Now that would never be. Nothing else much mattered.

Abigail did not go to work the next day. There seemed to be no point in it. There was not much point to anything now because she finally understood why Logan had never stopped his vendetta. She also knew that he never would stop. In helping Joe Saville she was not working to get things right for her father, she was once again working to Logan's plans, guided by his unseen hand.

In any case, she did not feel the need now to protect her father. She understood him too. All she wanted to do was go away and never think about it again. That would never be possible, though, not when she loved Logan so much. It would never be possible to run away from what was in her own heart.

She spent the day sorting out her things, getting ready to move from this house which had never really been home. The job had to be done carefully because she knew she would never again live here. To stay and meet her father daily was more than she could do. Every sight of him would remind her of the past, remind her of Logan and the bitter battle that had been fought for so long in such grim silence.

The next day at the office was her last. She knew that as she entered the wide swing-doors and her only feeling of regret was that she would never again see Martha and the people who had stood by her throughout the battle with Logan.

Martha was away from her desk and Abigail decided that the goodbyes could wait until later. She had no intention of staying in the office all day because she had too much to do at home. If her father should decide to leave his hospital and come home he would try to pressurise her into staying and she had no desire to argue with him. She would be gone by then.

'You're back, Mrs Steele.' Joe Saville greeted her warmly as she went into her office for the last time. He even managed a smile. 'There was a panic when you didn't show up yesterday. The whole place seemed to be holding its breath. As far as I can tell, the staff rate their chances of survival by your facial expression. It's difficult to imagine that the future of the Madden Corporation has depended on the warmth of one young lady.'

It seemed to be some sort of obscure compliment but if it was meant to reassure and please her it failed. Once more her guilty conscience surfaced, little devils of doubt driving their forks into her heart. She owed the loyal staff more than this. She was proposing to walk out, disappear entirely and yet even one day's unannounced absence had panicked them.

Abigail looked at him bleakly and his attempt at a sort of fatherly smile of approval faded.

'Are you ill?' he asked quickly. 'Can I get you anything?'

'No, thank you. I'm not ill,' Abigail muttered. She walked to the window and looked down at the street, keeping her back turned towards him. She knew it was now or never. This was her last and only chance to break free because, if she delayed, her father would be back, she would be pulled into things and every bit of her misguided loyalty and troubled conscience would work against her.

'I'm leaving.' Abigail spun round to face him. 'You don't need me here. You're running the place for Logan, getting it back on its feet. The staff will work for you and with you. They're the best. They're loyal and hard-working. At the moment I'm just a sort of mascot here and anything I can tell you can quite as easily come from Martha Bates. She was my father's secretary for years.'

'But I thought... Mr Steele said you were staying here, continuing with the firm even after I've finished my work.'

'No. I never agreed to that,' Abigail told him firmly. 'I promised to stay while you needed me but, in reality, you don't need me. In any case, I can't stay. I know things now that I didn't know when I offered to help you. I'm leaving today.'

'Does Mr Steele know?' Joe Saville asked a trifle anxiously, and Abigail managed a smile at the thought of this clever, talented man who was fast approaching late middle age being uneasy about facing the man who could take her to the very gates of heaven in his arms.

'He'll know when you tell him,' she pointed out quizzically, and he looked a trifle abashed.

'I'll have no choice but to tell him,' he confessed, glancing at her in embarrassment. 'I go over everything with him after I leave here each day and the first thing he asks is how you are coping. He even wants to know how you look.' He cleared his throat gruffly, his embarrassment growing. 'Mr Steele doesn't ask in a particularly kindly manner, you understand, but he asks all the same. He had to be away last night and he won't be back until this evening so I didn't have to tell him you were away from the office yesterday.'

'Never mind,' Abigail soothed ironically. 'You'll be able to make two astonishing reports together. One, I played truant yesterday, and two, I walked out today.'

'Do you have to?' he asked, and she nodded, collecting her things from the desk, methodically putting them into the box she had brought.

'I do if I want to survive, Mr Saville,' she said quietly.

CHAPTER TEN

ABIGAIL said goodbye to everyone, trying to reassure them as best she could. She held a small meeting in the staff dining room, trying her best to make it a very official parting and telling them that Logan was now guiding the firm to recovery. They already knew who Joe Saville was but as Abigail explained to them that Logan Steele was about to set the Madden Corporation back on its feet there seemed to be a collective sigh of relief.

There was not one person there who did not know Logan's brilliant reputation and there were quite a few who also knew why the Madden Corporation had plunged so steeply downhill. Several people were looking at her with pitying eyes but the heat was off and that was all they could see for the present.

Martha saw a little further, however.

'Has he stopped, Abigail?' she asked quietly when Abigail went to say goodbye privately.

'With the firm, yes. He gave me his word and that's good enough for me.'

'So why are you running for cover?' Martha asked. 'And don't bother to tell me that you're not. I've seen you fight for this firm, seen you nearly kill yourself in the attempt. You didn't run then but you're running now.'

'I fought hard because I was angry and because I had loyalty to my father,' Abigail said slowly. 'I have no anger left and no loyalty. I found out things I can't ignore. It's best that I simply go.'

'Where?' Martha asked. 'Will you work for Wingate's?'

'No.' Abigail shook her head, her eyes thankful. 'That's what I intended to do but now I can't. To be strictly truthful, Martha, I don't exactly know what I'm going to do. I have to think it all out. I'm just going away. I need time.'

She almost said that she needed space but she had said that to Logan. Now she would have all the space in the world because Logan would not be in her life. It would all be over. The final act. What he would do she didn't know. She didn't want to know. When some devastating blow fell she would no longer be connected to the Madden Corporation and she would not feel sorry for her father. Some people had bad luck for no reason at all. By inexcusable actions, her father had brought on himself any fate that Logan decided to deal out.

It was late by the time she had her things packed. Today was Rose's day off so she had no tiresome explaining to do. She hadn't given a thought to where she was going. All she wanted to do was run—run away from the truth, run away from the unhappiness. Where she went didn't seem to be very important.

On her drive back into London it gradually dawned on her that in spite of her despair she had to find somewhere to stay and she turned the car towards a row of quite respectable hotels she knew—small places where there was no glamour, no glitter, places that Logan's friends would never even know existed. Abigail knew, though. She had often pondered when she had first left Logan about how it would be simply to disappear, get away from her father, take on another character entirely. The hotels had looked secretive, inviting and cheap. She could call herself anything and nobody would know.

She pulled up outside one of them—the middle one—and went inside to see if there were any vacancies. Later she would get her things from her car. Then she would lock her door and sleep. Tomorrow she would think. Not now, not tonight. It was all so easy, so welcoming, and without any thought at all she signed the registration card in her own name, only realising too late that she had not meant to do that. Abigail Steele. It shouted out at her, made her nervous and she cast a quick glance at the man at the desk. He was not impressed by the name and she breathed a sigh of relief. She thought that Logan was omnipotent. Apparently, outside the business world, Steele was just another name.

Abigail went out to get her things, a very old porter accompanying her.

'It's no parking here,' he pointed out when he saw her car. 'It's OK across the road, after six and before eight in the morning. Later than that you'll have to find somewhere else. We don't have parking at the hotel. I should leave it across the road for tonight, though. It's late.'

It was. It was almost eleven and Abigail helped him load her cases onto a trolley and then left him to get them inside while she moved her car. The lateness of the hour hadn't really sunk in until he had told her but now she knew why she felt so deadly tired. It had been a long day, a bad day and all she wanted to do was sleep. She drove the car across to the other side of the road and reversed it into place, just managing to get it between two other cars.

At least it was legal until eight o'clock tomorrow. She locked up and looked across at the hotel. Now it didn't look quite so inviting. Nothing was inviting—nothing but the flat and Logan, the hard warmth of his arms and the smiling grey of his eyes. It was no use thinking about it, though. It was all gone for ever. Her own eyes clouded with tears and she stepped out across the road, only raising her head when lights blinded her and a horn screamed at her with a warning of terror.

The car had come round the corner at speed and she hadn't even looked. He was going too fast to stop and Abigail was hit by the front wing, tossed like a leaf against the parked cars, sliding to the wet, dark street to lie silent and lifeless.

She didn't know that the old porter had been watching her, worried about her safety at this time of night in a dark street. She didn't see the flurry of activity as he called for help and hurried across to her. The car had stopped and a white-faced young man was bending over her, frantically taking her pulse and shaking like a leaf himself when he could find no pulse at all.

'Leave her!' the old porter ordered fiercely, pushing him aside. 'You've done your worst.' He took off his jacket and carefully covered her, his hand stroking back the black hair from her face. 'Beautiful little thing,' he muttered. 'All by herself and so beautiful.'

Through the swirling mists of pain there were voices and, more and more, one voice dominated. It was a voice close to her, a voice she reached out for. It was huskily deep with a quiet desperation behind the words.

'Don't leave me, Abbie! Don't let go. You promised for ever. Don't leave me, darling.'

Other voices intruded; they were more controlled, not desperate. Cool hands touched her—efficient hands that took away the pain. Blackness returned, and nothing.

When Abigail opened her eyes finally, she saw Martha, the last touch of severity gone from her face, and Abigail tried to speak, tried to lift her head.

'No! Don't move. You're all taped up, Abigail. Moving can only hurt you. I'll come where you can see me better.'

Martha got up and came round the bed and even following the movements with her eyes hurt. Abigail lifted her hand and touched her face. There were no bandages although she could feel them round her head.

'You're not scarred, thank God!' Martha told her. She sat gingerly on the edge of the bed, watching for any sign that this would bring on pain. 'It was your head, your shoulders and your back.'

'How am I?' Abigail managed weakly, and Martha patted her hand.

'Fair to middling, love. Otherwise they wouldn't have let me creep in to see you. Until today it was only relatives, and that meant Logan.'

'Logan? He was here?' The distant memory of his voice came back but she knew it had all been a dream, the confusion of pain.

'He's been here for two days. He never slept, never left this bedside,' Martha told her firmly. 'They more or less threw him out this morning and he's gone to get a shower and a few hours' sleep. He wouldn't move until the doctor came and told him personally that you would be fine. You know what he's like. Even when he was dropping, he was the boss.'

'How did he know that...?'

'The police found him. You signed your name at that place you ran off to and they took one look at it and phoned him. He's been here ever since. Do you remember anything at all?'

'The car. I remember the car,' Abigail said slowly. Her eyes were beginning to close and she was too weak to fight the tremendous desire to sleep. Martha's voice droned on but Abigail didn't hear. In her head she was searching for another voice, for Logan's voice, trying to

remember the things he had said. It was all so much a
dream that she let it go and allowed herself to drift into
a sleep that painkillers thrust upon her.

When she came round again it was night, dimmed
lights allowing her eyes to open without any pain. Warm,
hard fingers held hers and she looked down wearily, her
eyes misting over when she saw the dark head that rested
against her hand. Logan was sitting beside her, his hand
still holding hers even though he had fallen asleep.

She slowly moved her fingers from his and her hand
lifted to touch his hair. Brown and gleaming, it fell over
his forehead, softening the harshly carved lines of his
face. He looked so tired, the thick black lashes casting
dark shadows against his cheeks, and she saw more vul-
nerability than she had ever seen in Logan. She stroked
his hair, wanting to soothe away the strain on his face.
It was terrible to love somebody so much and have no
right to show it.

'Logan.' She whispered his name to herself, a world
of longing in her voice, and he was instantly awake, the
grey eyes finding hers as she touched his face gently.

'Abbie!' He took her hand in his and cradled it to his
cheek. 'Abbie, my love. I'm sorry, so sorry.'

'I'm all right, Logan,' she whispered. 'It was not your
fault. Nothing was your fault. You don't have to pretend.
I know what happened. I know you couldn't either forget
or forgive. Now I know why you could never love me,
but it's all right, you don't have to pretend. At least I
had some time with you and I was happy.'

Pain crossed his face and the brilliantly grey eyes
darkened, the heavy black lashes blinking away the suspicion of tears.

'I *do* love you, Abbie,' he said deeply. 'I've always
loved you. Every minute away from you is a minute of
my life wasted. I tried to separate my life into two com-

partments. One was filled with your sweetness and the other filled with anger and bitterness. I wanted everything. I wanted you and I wanted revenge. Living like that could never have worked but I was too arrogant to realise it and I lost you. Now I nearly lost you for ever.'

Abigail managed a smile, her fingers curling round his.

'It was a stupid accident,' she said quietly. 'I was unhappy, not looking where I was going. I was running away.' She sighed shakily and closed her eyes. 'Nobody can really run away. It's not possible, is it?'

Her voice was slurred and Logan tightened his hand on hers.

'Don't leave me, Abbie!' he begged urgently. 'They said you were all right. You promised me a long time ago. You said, "for ever"!'

A smile touched her lips but her eyes didn't open.

'I'll promise all over again, Logan. For ever. I won't leave you if you want me.'

'I want you,' he assured her vibrantly. 'I love you, Abigail. Whatever it takes, I'll make things right.'

She just smiled and he raised her hand to his lips, entreaty still in his voice when he said, 'Don't sleep yet, Abbie. Just tell me I'm not imagining it. Tell me you love me.'

'I love you,' she whispered. 'I never stopped. Can I go to sleep now, please?'

Logan gave a brief, shaken laugh.

'Such sweet manners,' he said softly. 'You can sleep, my darling. I'll be here. Nothing in this world is going to hurt you.'

The next day Logan and Kent Madden walked in together and Abigail's stomach tightened with anxiety. They hadn't even seen each other since the day almost five

years ago when she had married Logan and the fact that
they had come together, or at least, arrived together,
was either unbelievable or a very nasty coincidence that
could only spell trouble.

'How are you, Abigail?' Her father came across to
her and Logan let him come first.

'I feel much better today,' she assured him, her glance
taking in his more healthy appearance. Her eyes slid ap-
prehensively to Logan and he smiled reassuringly as she
tried to concentrate on her father.

'You gave us a fright, Abigail,' her father said gruffly.
'I had no idea about the accident until—Logan let me
know.'

The slight hesitation in using Logan's name showed
how much of a strain this was for her father and Abigail
had no doubt that this meeting was not their first. Logan
had stamped his authority on things and he was here to
see that everything went according to his plan.

'Have you been here before?' she asked, and her father
nodded solemnly.

'Straight away, that first night. You were unconscious. I thought...' His voice trilled away and Abigail
was astonished at the emotion showing on his face. He
had never seemed to care for her but now he seemed to
be almost struggling with tears.

'Well, I'm all right now,' she said as briskly as possible,
and Logan came forward as if he could not bear to be
away from her for any longer.

'And you're going to stay all right,' he told her firmly.
'Next week I'll have you at home.' He smiled into her
eyes. 'This time I might just lock you in.'

'I won't be going anywhere,' Abigail said softly, and
for a second there was nobody else in their world as they
looked into each other's eyes.

'I want to give up the firm,' her father informed her in an emotional voice. 'He won't let me.'

'No, I won't,' Logan agreed stubbornly, his forehead creased in a frown. 'What the hell would you do with your time? It's no use appealing to Abbie either because I'm not having her bothered by petty details.'

'Not exactly petty—' her father began, but Logan stopped him at once.

'This is a new beginning. We have agreed on that already. That firm is the Madden Corporation and you'll run it. I'll help all I can but ultimately it's your responsibility. One day it will be Abigail's; you always intended that.'

'I did.' Kent Madden nodded his head and looked regretful. 'It's all I have to leave her. I always meant to train her but it all fell apart.'

'I tore it apart,' Logan stated with ruthless self-criticism. 'You can build it again and, as to Abigail, she needs no training if things are back to normal. According to Joe Saville, she knows exactly what she's doing.'

'I may not want to go back,' Abigail said quietly, and they both turned to her with slightly anxious eyes. 'It's all right,' she assured them. 'I'm not hanging onto the past and I'm not being bitter. It's just that I may want to simply be Logan's wife, have a family.'

'Then it's a legacy for your grandchildren,' Logan reminded Kent, his smile warm and tender as he looked at Abigail.

'It's something to work for,' her father said, and there was a little light in his eyes that gave Abigail hope for the future.

Two weeks later Logan came to take her home and he gave her a choice.

'The house or the flat?' he asked as he settled her carefully into the car and sat beside her.

'The flat,' she said with no hesitation. 'It all began there. It can start there all over again.'

'It never ended,' Logan said deeply, his eyes moving over her still pale face. 'When you left me, I stayed at the flat all the time. I couldn't bear to go to the house. We had so many plans for the place. I more or less hid in the flat, grimly hanging onto every memory of you.' He suddenly leaned across and pulled her into his arms, holding her tightly. 'God, I love you, Abbie!' he muttered thickly. 'You're the centre of my life. You have been since I first saw you.'

She looked up, her hand gently tracing his face as she saw every question answered by the look in his eyes.

'There never was Fenella, was there?' she asked softly, and he shook his head, his lips twisting ruefully.

'No, my darling. There was you from the moment I met you and there has never been anyone else.'

'Nor for me,' Abigail declared, and he smiled into her eyes, his warm looks melting her last anxieties.

'I know, sweet Abbie,' he assured her softly. 'In my heart I've always known. There was only ever you and me together, just as it was meant to be.'

Later, in the warmth of the bedroom, Abigail lay curled against him, her head on his shoulder, her eyes dreamily looking around the place where she had first belonged to him.

'You made a miracle for me,' she whispered, and Logan bent his head to trail his lips across her cheek.

'I can't make miracles, Abbie,' he said softly. 'I can only hang onto the one miracle I've got—a miracle I almost lost because of my bitterness.'

'I couldn't blame you,' she told him quietly. 'When Fenella told me, I was sure you could never have loved me at all. She told me about your father's suicide and—'

'It was an accident, Abigail,' he assured her firmly. 'There was something wrong with the car and he lost control. He would never have left my mother behind like that. They loved each other. I've known always that it was an accident but the rumours continued and I did nothing to stop them. It gave me even more reason to hate. I thought I could have everything. I thought I could keep you with me, locked away from the truth, and still continue my destruction. Kent is your father but I had no pity, no mercy.'

'Don't,' Abigail urged softly. 'It's over. He's back at work and he looks so different.'

'He's putting a good mind to straightforward action,' Logan grunted with a slightly irritated air, and Abigail wound her arms around him.

'Don't be angry,' she begged, and he relaxed immediately, turning towards her, his eyes roaming over her face.

'I'm not angry. I'll never be angry again. It's ironical to think, though, that if your father had run his business before as he's running it now I would never have been able to crush him.'

'Not even you?' Abigail teased, her wide green eyes mockingly innocent.

'Not even me,' he growled, tightening his hands on her. 'And don't look at me like that, not until you're quite well.'

'I am!' she protested, and he gave her a rueful smile.

'You're not well enough to soar off to the place you go to when I love you,' he said seductively. 'There are no half-measures with you, my love, and this baby can wait a little longer.'

'Will there be one?' she asked breathlessly, and he
pulled her back to his shoulder, his smiling lips against
her skin.

'Oh, there'll be one,' he murmured. 'Your desperation to have my children takes my breath away; be-
sides, you made a sort of promise to your father and
anyone called Steele lives by their word.'

'Why didn't we have one before?' she sighed, and
Logan wrapped his arms round her, holding her close.

'I thought you might get tired of me,' he confessed
softly. 'You were too young and I knew it. I couldn't
burden you with a child.'

'So it was my youth and your stupidity,' Abigail
taunted and he laughed delightedly.

'A fairly accurate summing-up,' he agreed. 'However,
don't get too accustomed to turning that sharp little
tongue on me. You won't always be too brittle to touch.'

Abigail looked out of the window, watching for the sight
of Logan's car. They had been back at the house for
two months now and it was wonderful to be in the place
they had planned together so long ago. Outside, the snow
was gently falling—big, fat flakes that had already coated
the garden and fields with a thick carpet of brilliant
white. It settled on the trees and hedges, softening an
already beautiful landscape. It was almost Christmas—
the first Christmas she had spent with Logan for four
years—and today the Steele Group closed down for the
holiday. She would have him to herself for a whole week.

She went back to the tall tree that stood beside the
glowing fire. Her daily cleaner had already left and she
had the quiet house to herself. She knelt down, carefully
putting the finishing touches to the decorations, her mind
drifting into the happy state she lived in now. Logan had
made things right as he had promised. Her father was

back at work, a changed man, and although there was still a slight hint of stiffness between Logan and Kent Madden they both tried hard to be normal.

Abigail knew it was for her sake but she had no worries. All of them had learned their lesson and that included her. She would never again doubt Logan's love. She heard him come into the hall and turned in surprise as he stood at the door of the drawing room, his eyes intently on her.

'I didn't hear the car!' she exclaimed, and he shook his head, his eyes never leaving her face.

'I parked round the back. It can stay there for the week because we're not going anywhere. I hope we get snowed in.'

He was so intense that Abigail blushed and it was only as his crystal-clear glance began to roam over her that she realised what was wrong.

'I found this when I was clearing the last of my things out to bring here,' she explained. 'It still fits. I thought it might surprise you.'

She looked down at the black skirt with red flowers that spread around her as she knelt, the red sweater that clung to her figure and made the blue-black shine of her hair more noticeable.

'You little devil,' Logan breathed. 'You knew exactly what it would do to me. It's like seeing you for the first time.' He dropped his briefcase on the floor and came across to her and Abigail laughed up at him as he towered over her. 'I hope this is not my Christmas present,' he said huskily, 'because I'm going to want a lot more than just the sight of you.'

He pulled her to her feet, his eyes searching her smiling face before his arms enclosed her gently.

'It's like going back with no unhappiness in between,' he whispered, his face against her hair. 'If I lost you now, darling, I don't think I could live through it.'

'You're never going to lose me,' Abigail said, winding her arms around his neck. 'I've learned to play my ace card. I know you love me. Nothing is going to make me feel insecure again.'

'You learn slowly but you learn well,' Logan complimented her as his smiling lips covered her own. He lifted her into his arms and walked out of the room, climbing the stair to their bedroom, teasing her with kisses all the way.

'You're not too delicate to touch now,' he reminded her as they finally lay locked together. 'We can just stay here. I don't need food.'

They looked into each other's eyes, so enthralled by their love that when Logan possessed her Abigail sped on swift, unearthly wings to her far-away place, only the dark sound of his voice holding her to earth.

He hovered over her when she came back, his grey eyes glittering, and she lifted her hand to touch his face.

'I love you,' she whispered in a trembling voice, and he turned his head to kiss her fingertips.

'I know. I never doubt it. I could stay here with you like this and never move for the rest of my life.'

'Martha and my father are coming to dinner,' she reminded him, smiling up at him with happy green eyes, and he rolled to his side, pulling her with him.

'I remember,' he growled. 'Is this when you tell them that you're pregnant?' He shot her an amused glance and Abigail sat up, staring at him in astonishment.

'I was just about to tell you! How did you know?'

'I was not born yesterday,' Logan assured her with mocking dignity. 'Sometimes I make the odd miracle just for myself.' He turned and pulled her down to him, grinning at her as she still watched him in awe. 'As a matter of fact,' he confessed, 'Dr Collingham stopped me as I was driving through the village. He offered his hearty congratulations.'

'He had no right!' Abigail pouted. 'I wanted to tell you myself.'

'So tell me,' Logan suggested huskily, and she threw her arms round him, her face alight with happiness.

'I'm having your baby! It will take me another seven months but I can wait if you can.'

'Oh, Abbie, my love,' Logan whispered, 'whatever you want, I want, but most of all I want you. Nothing should ever have parted us and nothing will ever part us again.'

'I should never have doubted you,' Abigail sighed. 'You were right, though. I was too young. I just dared not step into the battle between you and my father and when the rumours started about you and Fenella I believed them. Even when she was telling me about your father and mother she still insisted that you were—'

'My solicitor and nothing more,' Logan interrupted quietly. 'I gave her a choice when you were in hospital. She could leave or she could work in America. She chose America.'

'But you need her—don't you?' Abigail asked quietly, and he smiled down at her as he tucked her close.

'I need you. That's where it begins and that's where it ends. Nothing else matters.'

Nothing else would ever matter. Whatever went wrong they would put it right and they would do it together. The future had seemed empty but now it was filled with joy—the same joy they had felt in each other from the moment they had met.

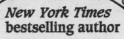

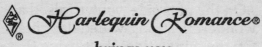

brings you

SIMPLY THE BEST

*Authors you'll treasure,
books you'll want to keep!*

Harlequin Romance just keeps getting better and better...and we're delighted to welcome you to our **Simply the Best** showcase for 1997, highlighting a special author each month!

These are stories we know you'll love reading—again and again! Because they are, quite simply, the best...

Don't miss these unforgettable romances coming to you in May, June and July.

May—GEORGIA AND THE TYCOON (#3455)
by Margaret Way
June—WITH HIS RING (#3459)
by Jessica Steele
July—BREAKFAST IN BED (#3465)
by Ruth Jean Dale

Available wherever Harlequin books are sold.

On the plus side, you've raised a
wonderful, strong-willed daughter.
On the minus side, she's using that
determination to find

A Match For
MOM

Three very different stories of mothers,
daughters and heroes...from three of your
all-time favorite authors:

GUILTY
by Anne Mather

A MAN FOR MOM
by Linda Randall Wisdom

THE FIX-IT MAN
by Vicki Lewis Thompson

Available this May wherever
Harlequin and Silhouette books are sold.

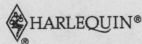 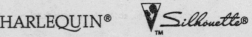